HEROES OF CHINA'S
GREAT LEAP FORWARD

HEROES OF CHINA'S GREAT LEAP FORWARD

TWO STORIES

EDITED BY

RICHARD KING

UNIVERSITY OF HAWAI'I PRESS
HONOLULU

Excerpts from earlier versions of the two stories published here first
appeared in *Renditions*, No. 68, pp. 52–76, 82–111. Reprinted by
permission of The Research Centre for Translation, The Chinese
University of Hong Kong.

LIBRARY OF CONGRESS CATALOGING-IN-PUBLICATION DATA

Heroes of China's great leap forward : two stories / edited by Richard King.

p. cm.

ISBN-13: 978-0-8248-3402-9 (hardcover : alk. paper)

ISBN-13: 978-0-8248-3436-4 (pbk. : alk. paper)

ISBN-10: 0-8248-3402-X (hardcover : alk. paper)

ISBN-10: 0-8248-3436-4 (pbk. : alk. paper)

1. China—History—1949–1976—Fiction. 2. Chinese fiction—20th century—Translations into
English. 3. Political fiction. I. King, Richard. II. Li, Zhun, 1928–2000. Li Shuangshuang xiao zhuan.
English. III. Zhang, Yigong. Fan ren Li Tongzhong de gu shi. English. IV. Title: Brief biography of Li
Shuangshuang. V. Title: Story of the criminal Li Tongzhong.

PL2658.E8H47 2010

895.1'35208—dc22

2009044046

Designed by Julie Matsuo-Chun

Printed by Sheridan Books, Inc.

CONTENTS

Introduction

1

A Brief Biography of Li Shuangshuang

LI ZHUN

15

The Story of the Criminal Li Tongzhong

ZHANG YIGONG

63

Glossary

129

INTRODUCTION

....

TWO CELEBRATED WORKS of fiction, written twenty years apart, present very different pictures of rural China in the late 1950s and early 1960s. This was the time of the Great Leap Forward, the utopian scheme designed to catapult China into the ranks of the world's leading military and industrial powers that instead precipitated the greatest famine of the twentieth century. Li Zhun's short story "A Brief Biography of Li Shuangshuang," of which the version translated here was published in 1960, shows the Great Leap Forward as it should have been, and was in the official press of the day: a time of hope, common purpose, and irrepressible energy that would liberate peasant women from drudgery into active participation in the life of the nation. By contrast, Zhang Yigong's short novel *The Story*

1

of the Criminal Li Tongzhong, dating from 1980, was among the first works to show a markedly less triumphal side to the Great Leap, portraying it as a time of hunger and heartless mismanagement, when Communist Party officials were willing to sacrifice peasant lives in order to impress their superiors.

The authors of these two works, Li Zhun (1928–2000) and Zhang Yigong (1935–) were both born and raised in Henan, the central Chinese province where the most grandiose plans for increasing production in the Great Leap were supported by mendacious accounting and followed by draconian grain levies based on gross overestimates of crop yields that led to mass starvation. Their fictional works, taken together, give a picture of the Great Leap's optimistic start and the tragedy that followed in one part of the country most terribly affected.

Each work is a superior example of the literary style of its time. "Li Shuangshuang" exhibits the "combination of revolutionary realism and revolutionary romanticism" introduced in the late 1950s to replace the Soviet doctrine of socialist realism from which it was derived; the Chinese formulation was designed to portray the nation's progress toward a glorious communist future in the most ideal terms, the world as it should be (from the point of view of the ruling Communist Party), and was about to become, rather than as it actually was. Fiction of the period offered images of heroic figures for a new age, young workers or peasants mastering new technologies and achieving prodigious increases in output, and (as in the present case) women emerging enthusiastically from the confines of the home to play a leading role in attaining the goals set by the national leadership. *Li Tongzhong*, written two decades later, is an example of the "Wounds" literature briefly prevalent in the years following the 1979 publication of the story from which the genre took its name.[1] Wounds literature focused on tragedies and injustices suffered in the recent past (usually the Cultural Revolution of 1966–1976, but occasionally the Great Leap Forward as well), that had been brought about by factional division within the Communist Party and ultra-leftist policies zealously applied by misguided or malicious officials, but the authors invariably expressed confidence that the new Party leaders and those rehabilitated officials who had been disgraced and imprisoned during the Cultural Revolution, would right the wrongs committed by their predecessors. The most common central characters of Wounds fiction are virtuous Communist Party officials who sacrifice themselves to uphold the true values of the Party, which their superiors are bent on subverting or destroying; in Li Tong-zhong's case, he takes the law into his own hands and feeds the starving at the cost of his position and his life.

The Great Leap and the Famines

The Great Leap Forward was launched in 1958 on the initiative of Chinese Communist Party Chairman Mao Zedong; it was his response to events both inside China and outside, principally in the Soviet Union. From the time Mao gained leadership of the Communist Party during the Long March in the mid-1930s until his death in 1976, his biography was inextricably linked with all the triumphs and disasters of the nation. Both those who, like the post-Mao rulers of China, regard Mao as a great leader who made serious errors and those who view him as a heartless tyrant can deploy the evidence of the Great Leap to support their cause.[2]

By the late 1950s the transformation of the system of ownership in the People's Republic had been completed: land was owned by state-controlled collectives rather than by individuals or families, and industry and commerce had been nationalized, allowing for the same sort of centralized management of the economy that was practiced in the Soviet Union. An attempt to elicit greater support from China's intellectuals for the development strategies of the Communist Party, by allowing greater latitude for expression in the Hundred Flowers movement in mid-decade, had backfired when the intellectuals used their newfound freedom to criticize the rule of the Communist bureaucracy as autocratic and stultifying. Mao's reaction was to launch the Anti-rightist campaign, which led to the condemnation and ostracization of hundreds of thousands of researchers, teachers, journalists, artists, and other intellectuals. The campaign reinforced the hostility many Party officials felt toward the intellectuals, and in addition the purges denied the state the expertise that might have argued against the more absurd projections and fantastic pseudoscience of the Great Leap. Beyond China's borders, the relationship between the Communist parties of China and the Soviet Union was deteriorating following the condemnation by the new Soviet leader, Nikita Khrushchev, of his predecessor Joseph Stalin. The two countries' uneasy alliance transformed into a bitter enmity, coupled with a rivalry for influence in the developing world. Since Mao now viewed the Soviet Union as a potential military threat, he felt even greater urgency to make China an industrial and military power in the shortest possible time, by accelerating the production of steel and developing the technology for an atom bomb.

Khrushchev had pledged that the Soviet Union would overtake the United States in the production of steel, and Mao resolved that China should surpass the United Kingdom by the same marker; this required a massive investment in heavy industry. New factories were built, and rural residents were brought in to staff them, doubling the size of the urban proletariat; scientists and technicians were redeployed to work on the Chinese atom bomb. At the same time, however, China was paying for the assistance that the Soviet Union had provided in the early 1950s, and it was also committed to providing food aid to selected countries in Africa, Latin America, and Eastern Europe.

The burden of feeding the burgeoning proletariat, meeting the demand for food at home and overseas, and even providing raw material for the new steel mills fell on China's peasants. The process of collectivization that had begun following the dispossession of the landlords and the redistribution of the land was completed with the establishment of the People's Communes; the peasants had been transformed from farmers of their own land to agricultural laborers producing for the state. Public canteens were set up to free women from domestic duties and increase the labor force for agricultural production and for construction projects that included reservoirs and dams. To produce iron, villagers were required to mine for ore, to operate hastily built "backyard furnaces," and even to give up whatever metal objects they owned; they also cut down trees to provide fuel to keep the furnaces burning. This expenditure of raw materials and human energy was unsustainable, but state and Party policies and quotas were rigorously enforced, with peasants being savagely punished by local officials if they failed to work the interminable hours demanded of them.

Those engaged in the production of grain were expected to achieve huge increases in harvests, based on the assumption that land could be made to yield as much as the grower dared to wish for. In pseudoscientific leaps of faith more extreme than those of Stalin's peasant agronomist Lysenko, peasants were told that deep digging and close planting would result in unprecedented levels of production and so dug through fertile topsoil and squandered seed grain in labor-intensive, wasteful experimental plots. A leading proponent of these fantasies was Henan's First Party Secretary Wu Zhipu, who claimed in 1958 that as a result of a philosophical leap forward on the part of the peasants of his province, rice paddies there had yielded seventy times as much as they had in the past. Communes were pressured into reporting incredible yields of grain, regardless of what was actually produced, and predicting even larger harvests to come. They were then taxed according to their inflated reports and false predictions, rather than the actual amount grown, which left them with little grain for food or seed. Mao appears to have allowed himself to be persuaded by the lies he was fed by Wu Zhipu and others, and by the staged demonstrations of bountiful harvests that he saw as he traveled the country on his private train. A plentiful supply of food seemed assured.

The famines began before the Great Leap's first year was out. The demand for labor in iron production and at construction projects left too few people to gather the 1958 harvest, and there was neither seed grain nor a workforce for the fall planting. When the canteens ran out of food, the peasants had no private plots to fall back on or kitchen utensils with which to cook for themselves. Guards were placed at granaries and on the trains that transported grain away from the countryside to protect it from theft by the people who had grown it. China's top leaders had to have known, from Party documents with an extremely limited circulation among the elite, of the suffering that the Great Leap was causing in the countryside, but they resolved to demand continued sacrifice rather than scale back on Mao's plans for modernizing the Chinese state. Not until 1962, with tens of millions dead in the countryside and food shortages threatening social stability in the cities, was the Great Leap effectively abandoned. Exports of food were halted, relief grain was imported from France, Australia, and Canada, and millions of the workers brought to the city at the beginning of the Leap were sent back to their villages. In the countryside, communes were permitted to close the public canteens (which most had done already when supplies ran out), and peasants were allowed to cultivate private plots to feed themselves. To avoid embarrassment to Mao and the Party leadership, the failure of the Great Leap was not admitted or addressed for twenty years, and even fifty years later the topic remains politically sensitive.

Li Zhun: Creating the Great Leap New Woman

A chance encounter in the late 1950s at a Henan village office with a local peasant woman provided the young author Li Zhun with the starting point for his most famous character, Li Shuangshuang, the feisty young wife who demands to take part in the excitement of the Great Leap, finds fulfillment in collective labor, organizes a public canteen, invents a new kind of noodles, and wins the heart of her conservative and formerly abusive husband in the process. The young woman Li Zhun met that day had come to complain to Party officials about her husband, whom she felt was too timid to meet the challenges of the Great Leap; when her tirade was interrupted by the ringing of the office telephone, she started shouting at that as well. Amused by her innocence and boldness, Li Zhun used her as one model for his heroine.[3] Shuangshuang's name, and her habit of leaving notes around the house to celebrate her progression toward literacy, came from a source closer to the author: his wife. Dong Bing, whose childhood name was Shuangshuang, attended classes in the 1950s, because she feared that her more educated husband, whom she married by family arrangement, would tire of her if she remained illiterate. While these two real women provided inspiration, they were not the only sources for Li Shuangshuang's forthright, humorous character: Li Zhun, who was far better read than his designation as a "village writer" implies, drew from earlier traditions as well. His heroine's swift repartee derives from the medieval story of the strong-willed bride Li Cuilian, who on her wedding day insults her own and her husband's parents, as well as others involved in the wedding, then threatens her husband with violence if he lays a finger on her, before she finally resolves to have nothing to do with any of them and goes to live as a nun.[4] Li Shuangshuang's tendency to sudden mirth recalls the charming fox fairy Yingning, the title character in a story in the eighteenth-century

7

collection of tales of the supernatural, *Strange Tales from Liaozhai* by Pu Songling, who giggles uncontrollably in unlikely and inappropriate situations.[5] Li Zhun did not admit these literary sources for more than thirty years after the story was written, because they might not have been thought suitable as models for a new socialist woman, but they add substance to the portrait of a woman who is resourceful, good-hearted, capable, and forceful —just the kind of woman the Communist Party needed to add to the labor pool for the Great Leap.

Li Shuangshuang, and the many works that bear her name, was the cultural success story of the Great Leap. The author believed that the story was reprinted over 400 times in numerous editions and read by 300 million people; in addition, the story was adapted as a comic strip and made into comic books, a film, and numerous local operatic forms. Throughout the many plot variations, the core of the story remained the same: the relationship between the spirited young peasant woman Li Shuangshuang and her much less progressive husband Sun Xiwang. Although the first version of the story was written in March 1959, the text translated here is the one that appeared in the premier literary journal, *People's Literature*, the following year. In both, Shuangshuang proposes setting up a collective canteen to allow maximum participation in the Great Leap by young wives. She takes over the canteen's management, to great acclaim, and invents a recipe for "Great Leap" noodles, made in part from sweet-potato flour, when wheat flour is in short supply. In the 1960 version of the story, the author has added Xiwang's miraculous training of the pigs to come when he plays their music on his reed pipe. The film *Li Shuangshuang*, with Zhang Ruifang in the title role, was made in 1962, after the demise of the public canteens, and the plot shifted focus to the allocation of work points, especially to women, in the new commune system. The movie adds a subplot in which a young couple choose each other as marriage partners despite the desire of the girl's parents to marry her to someone with more status than a peasant, which complements the story of Shuangshuang and Xiwang falling in love after marriage.

"A Brief Biography of Li Shuangshuang" is a story by a male author about female empowerment, where a pioneering woman proves herself a man's equal or superior in initiative, labor, and ideology and becomes more attractive in the process. Li Shuangshuang and her friends are capable of prodigious feats of labor, including entire nights of extra work, as well as social and technical innovation. The story is an affectionate portrait of both Shuangshuang and her husband Xiwang (whom the author claimed to have modeled in part on himself), peasants learning to be the kinds of people the new socialist society needed, and the author derives humor from their grappling with the new political vocabulary of the day. Now, almost half a century after the brief experiment with the canteens and the failure of the Great Leap, it is impossible to read the story without a sense of irony provided by knowledge of what awaited Shuangshuang and her neighbors in the future toward which she was rushing so blithely.

Zhang Yigong: Voicing the Donkey's Complaint

During the process of collectivization in the 1950s, which took the Chinese peasantry from individual farming at the outset of the People's Republic to the People's Communes in the Great Leap Forward, the novelist Zhang Yigong was working as a cub reporter; his assignment was to report on praiseworthy examples of the implementation of Communist Party policy and outstanding individuals who could serve as models for his paper's readers. His visits to villages where the collectivization policies were being implemented, however, told him that the peasants were not as enthusiastic about the process as the official media reported. One winter's night, after the inhabitants of one village had been ordered to turn over their privately owned livestock to the collective stock barn, Zhang was invited to participate in a modest act of rebellion: members of one family had decided to slaughter and eat their donkey rather than see it leave their possession. By the time Zhang arrived at the house where the feast was to take place, the carcass was already cooking in a gigantic pot. The animal's head was at the top, its jaws chattering together in the fiercely boiling water, in what Zhang imagined as a litany of complaint at the fate that collectivization had brought him.[6] Zhang has never retold this incident in his fiction, but it echoes in two places in *The Story of the Criminal Li Tongzhong*: first in the protest the central character infers from the last bellow of an ox slaughtered to feed the hungry villagers, and then in an absurd tale of animal dental hygiene the inventive village official Zhang Shuangxi fabricates in an attempt to satisfy the leadership's insatiable appetite for good news. Through the novel, the donkey finally speaks, adding its protest to those of the silenced peasants who perished in the famine years.

Like Li Zhun's heroine Li Shuangshuang, Zhang Yigong's hero Li Tongzhong is based in part on a real person: in the late 1950s, Zhang heard the story of a demobilized veteran whose lungs were damaged during the Korean War who was put in charge of a home for the elderly and disabled; when there was nothing for his charges to eat in the famine years, he arranged with the local peasants to steal from a public granary. This was not the kind of heroic tale his editors wished him to write, so Zhang simply noted it down. When the time came to write his novel twenty years later, he changed the disability from damaged lungs to a lost leg, and the position of the veteran to that of a local Communist Party secretary, and so created Li Tongzhong. Li Tongzhong is, like many central characters in early post-Mao fiction, both hero and victim, the model of what a Communist Party official should be who suffers for his virtue at a time when the Party has lost its senses.

The Story of the Criminal Li Tongzhong reads at times like a parody of the buoyant propaganda of the Great Leap period, including "A Brief Biography of Li Shuangshuang." The "Hot-shot" official, Yang Wenxiu, who is determined to advance his career by meeting the demands of his superiors whatever the cost to the peasants he controls, is reminiscent of Henan Province's First Party Secretary, Wu Zhipu, who claimed that political directives could result in massive increases in agricultural production. Wu's formulation of "The Philosophy of the Great Leap and a Great Leap in Philosophy" is parroted by Yang Wenxiu. The public expressions of triumph, including poetic eulogies, awards, parades, and public commendations, so common in the writing of the Great Leap era, are a source of bitter irony here, coming as they do while the majority of peasants are starving. The communal kitchens lauded in "Li Shuangshuang" are portrayed in *Li Tongzhong* as a failure, and successes in creating substitute foods from unlikely materials (like Li Shuangshuang's sweet-potato-based "Great Leap" noodles) are fraudulent, with the foodstuffs either made from the very materials they are said to replace or devoid of any nutritional benefit. Zhang Yigong loses few opportunities to mock the absurd claims made for the Great Leap by its proponents, and the succession of campaigns and public works projects that stretched the peasants to the limits of their endurance. Comic, even farcical, as *Li Tongzhong* can be at times, the overall tone is one of moral outrage and righteous anger. And while the new political terminology is a source of gentle fun in "Li Shuangshuang," as the modestly educated peasants learn the vocabulary of "leaping forward," "blooming and contending," and "retrogressionism," Zhang Yigong gives the words a sinister, even Orwellian, tone in his novel, where the rhetoric of progress is used to impoverish and punish the peasants.

Translating the Great Leap

The two translations here were made in collaboration with former students at the University of Victoria: "A Brief Biography of Li Shuang-shuang" by two recent graduates, and *The Story of the Criminal Li Tongzhong* by a group of upper-level undergraduates. Partial translations of earlier versions of both works appear in a special edition of the translation journal *Renditions* (Fall 2007); these sections are reproduced with the kind permission of the journal's editors, Anders Hansson and Bonnie S. McDougall, and include Bonnie McDougall's translation of the doggerel proverb on married life in "Li Shuang-shuang." I am indebted to the authors Li Zhun and Zhang Yigong for talking to me about their work and answering questions about the texts translated here, and to Dong Bing and Li Kewei (Li Zhun's widow and son) and Zhang Yigong for permitting their publication in translation. I would also like to acknowledge the contributions of my colleagues Lin Tsung-cheng, Tian Jun, Yvonne Walls, and Zhou Kefen with the translation; Michael Schoenhals for his comments on the glossary; and, for their generous and perceptive comments, the two anonymous readers invited by the University of Hawai'i Press to review the manuscript. I believe that the fiction of the Great Leap, both the optimistic stories written at the time and the later, darker, reconstructions of the era, is an indispensable part of the record of the initial euphoria, and subsequent despair, of that extraordinary time.

Notes

1. Lu Xinhua's story "Shanghen" (Wounds) was first published in the Shanghai newspaper *Wenhuibao* (Cultural gazette) on August 11, 1978, and was subsequently included in numerous anthologies. Two collections of translations of stories from this period are: Bennett Lee and Geremie Barmé, trans., *The Wounded: New Stories of the Cultural Revolution* (Hong Kong: Joint Pub-

lishing, 1979); Lee Yee, ed., *The New Realism: Writings from China after the Cultural Revolution* (New York: Hippocrene Books, 1983).

2. For the history of the Great Leap Forward, see: Jasper Becker, *Hungry Ghosts: China's Secret Famine* (London: James Murray, 1996). For the Great Leap in Henan Province, home to both Li Zhun and Zhang Yigong, see: Jean-Luc Domenach, *The Origins of the Great Leap Forward: The Case of One Chinese Province*, trans. A. M. Berrett (Boulder, CO: Westview Press, 1995). New research by Chinese and Western scholars appears in Kimberley Ens Manning and Felix Wemheuer, eds., *New Perspectives on the Great Leap Forward* (Vancouver, BC: University of British Columbia Press, forthcoming). For a biography of Mao as monster, see: Jung Chang and Jon Halliday, *Mao: The Unknown Story* (New York: Alfred A. Knopf, 2005).

3. I spoke to Li Zhun about his work in 1993, 1996, and 1998; much of the information about the writing of his story comes from those interviews.

4. For Li Cuilian, see H. C. Chang, "The Shrew," in *Chinese Literature: Popular Fiction and Drama* (Edinburgh: Edinburgh University Press, 1973), pp. 23–55.

5. For Yingning, see Denis C. Mair and Victor H. Mair, *Strange Tales from Make-Do Studio* (Beijing: Foreign Languages Press, 1989), pp. 73–89.

6. Zhang Yigong provided this memory, and other material on the story, in a 2002 interview.

A BRIEF BIOGRAPHY OF
LI SHUANGSHUANG

....

by Li Zhun

1

Li Shuangshuang is the wife of Sun Xiwang of the Sun Family Village Brigade of our commune, and is twenty-six or twenty-seven years old this year. Before the establishment of the commune and the Great Leap Forward, there were very few in the village who knew her name was Shuangshuang, because she already had two or three children when still very young. In the days of the agricultural collectives, she was seldom able to head out to the fields to do any work. Even when she put in a few days of labor during the busy season around the wheat harvest, these would all be entered

---

This version of "A Brief Biography of Li Shuangshuang" is dated February 2, 1960, late night. It was published in the March 1960 issue of *Renmin wenxue* (People's literature).

on Xiwang's work record. Among their village neighbors, when the elder generation mentioned her it was as "Xiwang's wife" or "Xiwang's woman," and the younger ones would just call her "Auntie Xiwang." As for Xiwang himself, in the past when he spoke of her in front of others he would just refer to her as "the one in my home," but in recent years, after she had children, he changed what he called her to "Little Chrysanthemum's mother." He also had another name for her that didn't sound as good, "the one that cooks for me."

Since she had so many alternative forms of address, of course the name Shuangshuang seldom made an appearance. But all things change in their due time, and in the spring of 1958 the Great Leap Forward allowed Shuangshuang to "leap" out. Not only did her name leap before the entire commune, it also leaped onto the pages of the county and provincial newspapers. The name Li Shuangshuang was pronounced resoundingly among the people. We must, however, take a step back. The first time her name appeared before the people was after the Spring Festival of 1958, on a big-character poster during a mass Blooming and Contending meeting at Sun Family Village. Our story must also begin at that point.

Early in the spring of 1958, the masses of the entire township broke with their traditions for celebrating the Spring Festival and launched a mighty drive to create an irrigation system.[1] Hoisting large flags and beating gongs and drums, the young men and women of Sun Family Village headed up Black Hill to build a reservoir. The workforce that was left in the village was kept busy gathering fertilizer and spreading manure, doing the spring hoeing, and planting sweet potato shoots. But because of the shortage of labor, there was just no way to take care of the wheat fields as well.

---

1. The Spring Festival, which comes at the Chinese New Year, is traditionally an extended holiday.

At this time, the commune's Party branch called on the masses to Bloom and Contend in discussion of this issue, asking everyone to come up with ways to solve the problem. A Mobilization Meeting was held at commune headquarters, and on the first day big-character posters were pasted up along the streets. That day Comrade Luo Shulin, the secretary of the township Party committee, came to Sun Family Village, and he and the commune's Old Party Secretary Uncle Leap read the colorful posters pasted up on the walls of the houses on both sides of the street. One poster in particular caught their attention.

The characters on this poster were oversized, and the handwriting was just a little crooked, but the content of what was written on it was exceptionally novel:

> Household chores
>   are such a bore!
> We've got the drive
>   but can't mobilize!
> If we're stuck home to cook all day,
>   how can Great Leap plans get under way?
> We have to start a canteen and then
>   we women will show we can take on the men!

The name signed at the bottom was "Li Shuangshuang."

Putting up this poster may not seem that big a deal, but Secretary Luo was thrilled with it. He read it out loud over and over again and slapped Uncle Leap on the shoulder: "Hey, old friend, we might just have something here! This poster is really important! If we can get the housewives out of their homes, then this Great Leap of ours could really take off!" Then he asked which household this Li Shuangshuang belonged to.

Uncle Leap thought about it and replied: "These young women

nowadays, I just can't keep track of them all. None of them come out to meetings that much."

"Go and make some enquiries," Secretary Luo said. "This is someone we have to pay a visit to and help bring her on. To be able to come up with something like this is not easy, it's really got some force to it!"

At the mention of "force," Uncle Leap said: "Now that you mention it, it's probably Xiwang's wife."

Secretary Luo asked: "How can you tell?"

Uncle Leap replied: "It's possible that young woman could come up with something like this. During the Great Contending last year, she went up on stage and gave a speech. It's just that she usually doesn't make it to many meetings. A couple of days ago I saw her scrapping with Xiwang."

As the two men were talking, the sun had worked its way directly overhead, and the shadows of the trees had shortened; people returning from the fields all gathered round to read the poster. Uncle Leap asked them: "This Li Shuangshuang, is it Xiwang's wife?" Some of them said it was, while others said it wasn't.

Someone said: "This was written by Xiwang's wife. During last winter's literacy campaign, Li Shuangshuang was the name she used to register at the community school."

Someone else said: "That young woman is smart as a whip and good at her studies, she could have written that."

Just as everyone was deliberating, Xiwang happened to return from the fields pushing a small cart. Xiwang is thirty-four, seven or eight years older than Shuangshuang. He also came from a poor background, and before Liberation he spent two years as an apprentice cook at a restaurant in the county town. But later, because he broke a couple of dishes when he was serving food and was afraid of being beaten by the manager, he skipped town and drifted around with a musical troupe for a couple of years, only getting back to the village after Liberation.

Everyone saw Xiwang and called out: "Xiwang, who do you think wrote this big-character poster? Could it be your Little Chrysanthemum's mother?"

When Xiwang heard that Shuangshuang had pasted up a big-character poster, his first reaction was alarm. He thought to himself: "That fool never thinks before she acts. She'd better not have let on about that fight we had a couple of days ago!" Seeing both Secretary Luo from the township and the Old Party Secretary there reading the poster, he was all the more reluctant to admit to it. Hemming and hawing, he walked over to the poster and read it over, and he felt as relieved as if a stone had been lifted from his heart. Again he heard Secretary Luo exclaim: "Well written! This poster is really well written!" He finally mumbled: "Yes, that was written by the one who cooks for me."

As soon as Xiwang's words were out, everyone exploded with laughter. Xiwang thought they were laughing at him for bragging about his wife, so he hurriedly provided confirmation: "You don't believe me? It really was written by my Little Chrysanthemum's mother. Her name is Li Shuangshuang, and she knows how to write! She doesn't just put up big-character posters here, she's always scribbling little notes. They're pasted up all over our house." As he said this, the crowd laughed even harder. Chuckling, Secretary Luo asked him: "And just what does she usually write on those little notes?"

Xiwang blushed: "She's just a woman, what does she know. She writes stuff like what's on this poster: 'I really want to study, but I just don't have the time,' 'When will I be able to stop cooking and participate in the Great Leap?' Then there's: 'The character for trousers, *ku* 裤, take out the part that means clothing, *yi* 衣, and it becomes the character for reservoir, *ku* 库' . . . all sorts of things! They're pasted all over the head of the bed, on the window papers. I can't remember what they all say. Anyway, that one who cooks for me, she's all talk, she's got no sense of the effect what she says can have. You don't need to take any notice of her." As he was speaking, Xiwang went to tear the poster Shuangshuang had written from the wall, but the Old Party Secretary held him back: "Just what do you think you're doing? She's written a poster, and you think you can just tear it down? She's Blooming and Contending!"

When he heard this was Blooming and Contending, Xiwang quickly pulled his hand back. Secretary Luo looked him over and chuckled: "Xiwang, my friend, your wife Li Shuangshuang's poster is excellently written. Her suggestion will be really useful for our entire township's Great Leap Forward. It's not the case that she doesn't know anything, actually she knows a great deal. I'm going to take this poster with me. The township Party Committee will hold a special meeting to discuss this idea." Patting Xiwang on the shoulder, he continued, "*Ai*, and from now on you have to change your old ways. Why do you always call her 'the one who cooks for me'? Her posters are pasted at the head of your bed, shouldn't you be a bit more democratic?"

When Secretary Luo had finished speaking, he took down the poster, folded it up and put it in his pocket, then headed off to commune headquarters with the Party secretary. For the moment, Xiwang was struck dumb, unable to make head or tail of anything.

2

Xiwang was deep in thought as he headed for home, pushing his empty wheelbarrow.

He thought, that woman of mine writes a couple of lines of doggerel, and the township Party Secretary Luo thinks that what she wrote is a thing of great value! But this is pretty risky too. It's just as well she didn't let on about that fight we had. If she'd really written a big-character poster about me and stuck that up by the roadside, it's likely everyone would have been "disputing" with me! *Ai*, with an outspoken woman like that, I'll have to be a bit more careful in the future.

Actually there was a whole series of reasons for the fight that Xiwang and Shuangshuang had had a couple of days before. Shuangshuang's family had been destitute peasants before Liberation, and she had been given in marriage to Xiwang the year she turned seventeen. For the first few years after she came into his house, Shuangshuang was just a kid, she didn't know anything about anything, and she got beaten by Xiwang on a regular basis. After the Land Reform, the government implemented the new marriage law, and Xiwang didn't dare hit her all the time. For one thing, life was getting a bit better, and he was afraid she would divorce him; for another, now that Shuangshuang had the children, she had more of a temper than before. Sometimes when Xiwang hit her, she would fight back for all she was worth. Xiwang had picked a fight with her a couple of times and hadn't been able to get the better of her. The village cadres criticized him for his unreasonableness, and after that he hadn't used his fists on her. He was still in charge of the affairs of their family, at home and outside. With collectivization, the principle of equal pay for equal work was brought in, and although Shuangshuang didn't work that much, she still received a share. Xiwang was supposed to consult her whatever he did, but Shuangshuang had the children to look after and so didn't go to many meetings or get out to the fields much. Xiwang was happy to put in a little extra work himself; from his point of view, it saved him a good deal of trouble.

Xiwang actually did like Shuangshuang. He liked her fiery personality, and he liked the way she had turned into someone with a forthright nature, always daring to talk and laugh. Shuangshuang was good-looking, skilled with a needle, and quick and neat about her work. In recent years she'd been able to spin half a pound of thread a day from the coarsest of cotton fibers, and she could weave thirteen or fourteen feet of cloth in a day. Even now when there were more children,

Xiwang never went without new cloth shoes, and the children always had clean cotton-padded clothing to change into when the wind turned cold in the autumn. But there were also things about her that Xiwang didn't like, such as that in his opinion she talked too much, and she tended to mind other people's business and talk about things that did not concern her. Because she was interfering, she inevitably got into fights with people, so that sometimes Xiwang had to make apologies for her. Whenever this sort of thing happened, Xiwang would always angrily lament: "*Ai*, that woman of mine is just too quick-witted. If she wasn't so smart, she'd be easier to get along with."

The winter before last, the village expanded the community school and Shuangshuang enrolled. While at school she concentrated on her studies and didn't get into as many quarrels, which meant that Xiwang could relax. He thought to himself: "This is fine, she can learn to write a couple of characters a day, and it will keep her mind occupied. After all, everyone needs to have an interest."

When the village provided each household with access to a radio broadcasting network a couple of years earlier, Xiwang had installed a loudspeaker. Xiwang enjoyed listening to the local *bangzi* opera and music played on the *suona* reed pipes, while Shuang- shuang preferred news and reports. With each of them taking turns, things went along quite smoothly. But Xiwang hadn't anticipated that with Shuangshuang getting an education, and then listening to news broadcasts and reading newspapers, she would stir up more trouble. Not only was she posting up little notes all over the house, she had even got into a fight with Xiwang a couple of days before.

The fight happened on the seventh day of the first lunar month. Shuangshuang watched as all the young villagers headed up to the reservoir on Black Hill. She had heard that they were also going to redirect Red Rock River into the village and were digging a large irrigation channel east of the village. She put in a request to go and work on the channel.

Xiwang said: "Forget it. The team didn't assign you any work there."

Shuangshuang replied: "Assigned or not, I still want to go. I'm bored stiff stuck at home. Everyone is out there taking part in the Great Leap Forward, and I can't even leave this house!"

Xiwang said: "What's all this about a 'Great Leap Forward'? They're just digging."

Pursing her lips, Shuangshuang glowered at Xiwang and said: "Enough of your conservative talk, I'm going!"

Xiwang couldn't change her mind and just had to do as she wanted, taking the children round to their neighbor Fourth Auntie, while Shuangshuang went off to the east of the village to work digging the irrigation channel.

After a couple of days' work, Shuangshuang's cheeks were rosy from the wind, she was more talkative and laughed more loudly, but she was also busier than ever, especially with having to cook three meals a day. She had to race home before quitting time and hurry to prepare a meal while the fire was still smoky. Before the food even reached her mouth, the bell from the team would ring to summon them back to work.

At noon on the seventh day of the lunar month, Shuangshuang returned home a little late, and as she came in, she saw the children crying for food. She was utterly exhausted, and with the children yelling, Shuangshuang got really flustered. She parted the curtains hanging in the doorway and went into the house to have a look, only to find Xiwang already home and lying on the bed having a smoke.

Seeing this made Shuangshuang furious: "The kids are crying like this, and you don't take care of them? It's all very well for you to take it easy!"

But Xiwang just puffed on his pipe, not saying a word.

Shuangshuang took two steamed buns out of the basket and gave them to the children, washed her hands, and then kneaded the dough: "It's not like you can't cook. When you get home just get the dough ready ahead of time, and I'll roll it out when I get back. This will save some time. All you do is lie on the bed and smoke!"

At that, Xiwang extended two fingers to dismiss this idea: "*Ai!* I couldn't do that. Cooking is a woman's job. If I cook for you now, before you know it you'll be getting me to wash diapers!"

Shuangshuang's heart seethed with anger: "You need to realize the difference between being busy and being idle. Haven't you noticed how busy I am?"

Xiwang replied: "You've brought this on yourself. I can't be looking after you."

As she sliced the dough into noodles, she rapped the cutting board with the knife and snapped: "When we turn the commune's dry fields into paddy fields, don't you bother eating any of the food we grow."

Xiwang retorted: "So you're saying you don't want to let me eat! That's fine! But in the future it's still going to be you who has to cook for me."

Shuangshuang's eyes flared. She threw down the knife with a clang: "Eat! You won't get to eat!" And with that, she slumped down furiously on the doorstep and began to cry.

While Shuangshuang sat there in tears, Xiwang acted as though nothing had happened. He lay down for a while and then, with studied unconcern, he went over to the chopping board to look at the noodles Shuangshuang had sliced. "This is enough for me, I'll cook them myself," he said, walking over to the pot and dropping in the noodles. While the noodles were boiling, he found a couple of cloves of garlic, minced them with a knife, added a little vinegar, and got ready to eat his dish of noodles.

Inside the house, Shuangshuang's wailing became more anguished as Xiwang pounded away at the garlic.

Shuangshuang ground her teeth as she watched him prepare the noodles so casually, thinking to herself: "Here I am here crying, while you're there eating. You won't get your fill!" At that point, she rushed over and delivered two vicious punches to Xiwang's spine.

After taking these two blows, Xiwang yelled: "Fine! You asked for it!" Grabbing the garlic pestle, he turned and was about to hit her back when Shuangshuang grabbed hold of him and gave him a shove that pushed him out of the house and left him sprawling on the ground in the courtyard.

Once she'd pushed Xiwang to the ground, Shuangshuang couldn't keep herself from bursting out laughing. She laughed so hard she shook the tears off her face and onto the ground.

Xiwang pulled himself up off the ground and was about to explode when Shuangshuang came over and grabbed hold of him: "Let's go! We're going to get the Old Party Secretary to sort this out! You think you can get away with this? I'm taking part in the Great Leap Forward, but you don't want me to. All you care about is your own comfort, and you're purposely making it hard for me. What kind of thinking is that! Let's go!"

Xiwang had wanted to give Shuangshuang a couple of really good whacks, but when he heard what she said, he knew he was in the wrong. Besides, he really had been trying to make life difficult for Shuangshuang. So he didn't dare to hit her again, much less go to see the Old Party Secretary with her. He quickly pulled his hands away and, standing right in front of the door, said angrily: "Go on! You go there first and I'll follow!"

That may have been what he said, but actually he just slipped away.

3

Their scrap left Shuangshuang feeling both angry and amused. There was, however, actually something else on her mind. She thought to herself: "Just fighting like this is no use at all. I have to come up with something better."

That night, after Shuangshuang got the children to sleep and adjusted the wick on the lamp, she sat alone by the window stitching soles for cloth shoes and thinking about what was bothering her. Then suddenly, light from a fire east of the village turned the window paper a glowing red. Like raindrops, the sounds of pickaxes and shovels digging into stone pattered in the distance, interspersed with bursts of excited shouting and laughter from the villagers.

Shuangshuang peered eastward through the window, knowing it was the night shift on the Red Rock River irrigation project. Lanterns were strung out in a row, like a fiery dragon; the lanterns lit up a long line of dark figures, their pickaxes and shovels in constant motion, rising and falling. The pounding of stone sledgehammers beat out a rhythm, while the clear voices of young men and women singing work songs flowed like a tide that swept through the window into Shuangshuang's home.

"The Great Leap Forward is turning the sky red outside," Shuangshuang thought, "Can I let myself be tied down by this household for the rest of my life?" She felt her heart race and her cheeks burn and was no longer in the mood to work.

Just then, the door creaked open, and somebody came in. Shuangshuang assumed it was just Xiwang and purposely refused to look.

"*Yo!* You're putting on airs, ignoring me like that! Or are you nodding off?"

Shuangshuang quickly looked up to see Guiying,[2] the wife of Changshui from the South Courtyard. Laughing, she said: "I thought it was my Lord and Master returning home, but it's you!"

---

2. Guiying shares a given name with Mu Guiying, a celebrated woman warrior of historical mythology; Mu Guiying is said to have replaced her husband as an army commander after his death.

Guiying said: "What's up, don't you want to see him?"

Shuangshuang replied: "I don't want to have anything to do with him for the next ten lifetimes!"

"Don't be like that," said Guiying, "Haven't you heard the proverb?"

> Like rain from the sky that sinks into the soil,
> Couples who quarrel make peace as they toil.
> They eat from the same pot when day's work is done,
> Then on the same pillow two heads lie as one.

Shuangshuang retorted: "We're not even able to eat together!"

As the two women spoke, they began to giggle, making so much noise that the children began to toss and turn in bed. They quickly suppressed their laughter.

Shuangshuang softly asked Guiying: "How about your kids?"

"I just got them to sleep too," said Guiying.

"Why aren't you in bed?"

"Can't sleep. What about you?"

"I can't sleep either," Shuangshuang said, "I heard that in a few days the water in the irrigation channel will flow right by the village."

Guiying said: "Auntie Xiwang, tell me, what are people like us going to do? Everyone else is Leaping Forward, but how are *we* going to make a Great Leap? The day before yesterday my husband, Changshui, went to the reservoir on Black Hill. I wanted to go too, but he said people like us with children aren't allowed. I told him I would go to the reservoir to cook, but he said there'd be nobody to look after the children!"

Shuangshuang stood up suddenly and asked: "Have they set up a canteen at the reservoir?"

Guiying replied: "Sure. The day before yesterday they took all the big pots and steamers up there with them."

Shuangshuang threw down a shoe sole: "*Hei*! If they can set up a canteen at the reservoir, why can't we have a canteen in the village?" Clapping her hands, Guiying said: "Yeah! Now that's an idea!"

As the two young wives cheered up, they became more energetic and resourceful. They discussed how they would run a canteen and how they could make arrangements for their children. The more they talked, the more enthusiastic they became, chatting well into the night. Still not satisfied, Shuangshuang dragged Guiying off to find the Old Party Secretary that very night.

They arrived at his home before he got back from the worksite; Auntie Leap was the only one at home. When they mentioned that they wanted to set up a canteen in the village, Auntie Leap said: "You two have come up with this at just the right time. There is a meeting being held tonight to investigate how to get more people into the workforce. Your idea is great! Bring it up, go ahead and Bloom and Contend, it's sure to go over well!"

Shuangshuang asked: "But how are we going to Bloom and Contend?"

Auntie Leap replied, "Paste up a big-character poster! You can both write. Take your idea, write it out in big characters, and paste it up in the street if you want!"

While Auntie Leap was still speaking, Shuangshuang grabbed hold of Guiying: "Come on! Don't bother what anyone says. We'll worry about what happens after we've pasted it up!" Full of enthusiasm, the two women headed out.

Shuangshuang got home to find Xiwang already fast asleep. She lit the lamp again, found a sheet of paper, and began writing out her big-character poster. As she was writing, Xiwang woke up to see Shuangshuang concentrating intently on what she was writing. He called out to her: "*Wei*! Get to sleep. Don't stay up all night. It doesn't matter how many characters you write out, you're never going to be a scholar!"

Shuangshuang just ignored him and focused on her writing. She wrote until the light was rising in the east before she finally had her *kuaiban* rhyme written.[3] Then she took it out and pasted it up by the road.

It had never occurred to Xiwang that the big-character poster Shuangshuang wrote would be of such value.

After he had pushed his empty wheelbarrow back home, he sat in the courtyard and giggled like a fool as he looked at Shuangshuang. Shuangshuang became impatient with his laughing and told him off: "Just what are you giggling at? You're sitting there laughing like you've eaten a clucking chicken and started clucking yourself!"

Xiwang made a face: "Little Chrysanthemum's mother, you're a hard one to figure out."

"What are you talking about 'hard to figure out'? If you have something to say, just go ahead and say it. Quit beating around the bush!"

Xiwang said: "That big-character poster of yours caught the eye of Secretary Luo from the township, and he said the rhyme you wrote is really important. The township Party Committee is going to hold a special meeting to discuss it."

"Really?" Shuangshuang was so happy she was practically jumping for joy.

But Xiwang continued: "I'm telling you, in the future try not to make so much trouble for me! You can't just paste posters up whenever you feel like it. What do you understand about policies! What kind of an idea is this canteen business? Can the commune just open up a restaurant?"

Shuangshuang replied: "All you can think about is running a restaurant. What I'm talking about is setting up a public canteen

---

3. *Kuaiban* (clapper song) is a form of poetry that can be recited to the rhythmic accompaniment of hand-held clappers.

where all the households in the village pool their food supply, and a couple of talented cooks are selected to make meals. Just like up there at the reservoir, it will save manpower and fuel. As for you, my good man, in the future don't even think about trying to make things hard for me. I'm not just going to obey you blindly any more. I've had enough of that."

Hearing her say this, Xiwang forced a laugh: "It sounds to me like you want to grow wings and fly away! How is that going to work? A bunch of families eating together, that's something different! If the township approves that poster of yours, huh . . ."

Shuangshuang said: "It's not certain yet, but if they want to go ahead with it, what are you going to have to say about it?"

Xiwang said: "If they go for your idea, I'll walk around in circles on my hands!"

Before Xiwang had finished speaking, the speaker hanging from eaves of the house started up. The broadcast began: "Good news to report to all commune members! In order to get us Leaping Forward even more, and based on a request from the masses, the township Party Committee will establish a mass public canteen in Sun Family Village. . . ."

Hearing these words, Shuangshuang was so delighted she took off at once toward the street. As she reached her doorway a group of women including Auntie Leap, Fourth Auntie, and Guiying were surging toward her house shouting and yelling: "Shuangshuang! Our big-character poster worked! The township wants us to start a canteen!"

"Let's go, we've got to find a place to build a stove!"

"Who knows how to build a stove?"

"There's an ideal person! Xiwang! He knows how. He can set up a big powerful stove!"

"We have to borrow a big pot. The Ermao family from the eastern side of the village has a big pot they used when they slaughtered cattle!"

Within moments, the Xiwang family courtyard was as thronged with people as though they were rushing to a New Year's gathering. A noisy group of women, laughing and shouting, dragged Xiwang off in search of a place to set up the stove.

4

A location was found for the canteen to the south of the village crossroads, in the courtyard where the wealthy middle peasant Sun You's family used to keep their carts. They whitewashed the three north-facing rooms a sparkling snowy white, and they built two large coal-fired cooking stoves under the window on the southern wall. Two big cast-iron vats were placed on the stovetop, while on either side sat a pair of cooking pots, each as big around as a bull's girth. Then, at the eastern end of the room, they put together a twelve foot by eight foot chopping board made of persimmon wood.

After they had borrowed all the hardware and utensils they needed, the Sun Family Village Agricultural Cooperative Mass Public Canteen was ready for the fires to be lit in the stoves.

Within the courtyard over a hundred families had gathered at the new canteen premises to select the canteen's cooks and superintendent.

During the meeting the Old Party Secretary talked about how the Township Party Committee supported everyone's request to set up a canteen and that this suggestion had been acted on as soon as it was raised. When it finally came around to selecting the kitchen staff, everyone erupted in a noisy clamor.

Shuangshuang was the first to speak. Her face blushing red, she shouted: "*Wei*! I propose we call on Fourth Auntie to be a cook. Fourth Auntie is a poor peasant, she's neat and tidy and reliable in her work. Not only that, we all know Fourth Auntie's heart's in the right place!"

As soon as Shuangshuang finished speaking, the crowd cried in support: "Fourth Auntie's our first cook! She can do it!"

"She certainly won't waste any rice or noodles."

"The pots and steamers here are all big and heavy. We still need somebody big and strong."

"Let's pick a man this time!"

Xiwang was at the meeting that day. He'd come by to watch and was off to one side puffing on his pipe, and certainly hadn't expected anybody to bring up his name . . . but Guiying did.

Guiying stood up and made a suggestion: "*Ai*, I've got somebody. Brother Xiwang. We all know that Brother Xiwang is an ace in the kitchen. He used to work in a restaurant. Stir fry or quick fry, he can do it all. But we've never actually seen him cook! What do you say, everyone?"

"Right," the crowd responded in agreement. Someone added: "With someone as strong as he is working in the canteen, fetching water won't be a problem!"

"With Xiwang working here, if we want to eat chicken or fish, nothing will stop us!"

"Xiwang will be great, he's a good guy." The wealthy middle peasant Sun You hadn't been very keen on the idea of a canteen to start with, but after hearing what everyone had to say, he also expressed his agreement.

Someone from the crowd continued: "With Xiwang doing the cooking for the canteen, even the turnip dishes will be tasty."

Everyone in the crowd chipped in, all of which delighted Shuangshuang. In all the time since she'd been married to Xiwang, she had never seen so many people praising him. She thought to herself: "This Great Leap Forward is really making good use of people's skills. Just look at all the support Xiwang's getting."

Just as she was thinking this, Xiwang stood up to speak. He seemed very full of himself. Instead of smoking his pipe, he pulled a cigarette from behind his ear and cleared his throat a couple of times before speaking: "Everyone has just nominated me to go and work in the canteen, but I can't do this kind of canteen work. I know people will say, 'You used to work in that restaurant at Cedar Inn in the North Mountains, so this village canteen of ours would be no problem for you.' But that's exactly the reason. It's just as people say, you can only understand what's written down if you've studied the right books. The apprentices at the restaurant were separated into the bun-and-noodles section, the cooked-dishes section, and the food-prep section. I studied in the cooked-dishes section. If you want chicken or fish, I can do it steamed or braised. But steaming buns and making noodles, that was a different section. . . ."

Xiwang had not finished what he was going to say when the crowd shouted out, "We picked you because you know how to cook!"

"If you can work a grinder, you can turn a millstone; it's all the same kind of work! It won't be long before we'll have fish and chicken to serve in our canteen, you have to look ahead!"

"The fish in the reservoir are all over a pound!"

At that moment Shuangshuang laughed and pointed at Xiwang: "He knows how to steam buns. He also knows how to make noodles. At home he often makes himself a snack if he feels like it."

Realizing Shuangshuang had called his bluff, Xiwang glared at her: "You've got some mouth on you! When have you ever seen me cook for myself?"

Not letting up, Shuangshuang replied, "You just cooked the other day! How can you say you don't know how to make noodles or steamed buns? You're being honored, but you won't accept it. I can't stand people who 'won't go forward when they're dragged, and go the wrong way when they're hit,' people who say they're 'dog meat and not good enough to be set on the table.'"

Shuangshuang's cutting remarks elicited great laughter from the crowd at the scene. Xiwang rolled up his sleeves as if wanting to say something more, but then the Old Party Secretary took over: "The establishment of this canteen is for the benefit of all commune members. It's to allow our commune's production to Leap Forward even further. If we're selected by everyone, it's because people think we can be of service. We can't go turning it down."

Even though the Old Party Secretary didn't say much, every word of it was aimed at Xiwang. Xiwang was often self-important, but he was extremely deferential toward the Old Party Secretary. He blushed: "In that case, ignore what I just said. You can take the word of the one who cooks for me."

As soon as these words left his mouth, the crowd erupted in laughter, and even the Old Party Secretary had to laugh. Blushing scarlet, Xiwang scratched his head, realizing that this form of address really was behind the times!

5

The first meal served in the canteen was sorghum and green beans with noodles, a dish known as "carp flitting through the sand." Because it was the canteen's inaugural meal, both the Old Party Secretary and Team Leader Yushun were personally on hand in the kitchen.

As for the cooks, Guiying had been chosen along with Xiwang and Fourth Auntie. They hadn't been able to find a superintendent for the time being, so this responsibility was given to Sun You's adult son, Jinqiao. Jinqiao had graduated from primary school, but later, because of his age and his failure to pass the middle school entrance examinations, he had to work in the commune. That day, the Old Party Secretary arrived at the canteen early and got a fire going. He then grabbed a shoulder pole with water buckets and hurried back and forth filling up the water vats. Watching the Party secretary work so hard at his advanced age made Xiwang feel a little guilty.

After he had rolled out a few lumps of noodle dough, he passed them on to Guiying and the other women to be cut, and took the Old Party Secretary's carrying pole and water buckets and went off to fetch water. He hauled more than thirty loads of water without taking a break, filling the two large vats to the brim before he considered his work finished.

When it was time to eat, the entire village—men, women, old and young—all came to the canteen. Shuangshuang also brought her three children, Little Chrysanthemum, Little Whistle, and Little Reed Pipe. She watched Xiwang wearing his chef's hat and his snow-white uniform embroidered with large red characters as he rushed about serving people and taking their meal tickets. Everyone was calling out to him and searching him out; it looked as if he could laugh and chat with them all, as though he was suddenly ten years younger.

While they were eating, Shuangshuang glanced over at him from a distance and smiled. She made a point of lifting the noodles high out of her bowl and into her mouth and called over to him appreciatively, teasing him, as if to say: now I can eat food *you* prepared! Xiwang saw what she was up to, but turned away and pretended not to notice.

Before the Old Party Secretary had his meal, he went from table to table asking everyone for their opinions about the canteen. He approached Shuangshuang and asked: "Shuangshuang, is the food in this canteen any good?" Laughing, Shuangshuang replied: "It's excellent! And this saves so much time. When you've finished eating, you just wipe your mouth and go. Now we can just focus on Leaping Forward, with nothing to fuss or worry about!" As she spoke, she looked at Xiwang, and he thought to himself: "Okay then, so now you're really a somebody!"

When the meal was over, Xiwang cleaned up the canteen and returned home. He saw that Shuangshuang was looking after their two boys Little Whistle and Little Reed Pipe, washing their faces, putting on powder and face cream, and changing their clothes before sending them off to kindergarten. Xiwang entered the room but ignored all the fuss. Letting out a long, deep sigh, he said, "Goddamn, all that work is really killing me. My whole body is just exhausted." And as he spoke, he collapsed onto the bed.

Shuangshuang knew that he liked to boast about how much work he had done, and so she just ignored him, letting him sit there moaning and complaining all the time. When the children were all ready to go, Auntie Leap, the head of the kindergarten, came by to pick the boys up. After they were gone, Shuangshuang returned to the room and poured a glass of hot water from the thermos. She pursed her lips into a smile and with both hands carried the glass over to Xiwang, placing it in front of him.

"Are you worn out?" she asked softly.

"Feels like my spine's been pulled out," exaggerated Xiwang, putting on his most long-suffering face. Shuangshuang prepared a basin of warm water and carried it over to Xiwang, chiding him: "Just look at your face, all smeared with dirt so you look like General Jingde in the operas! You're always going on about how you worked in a big fancy restaurant, but you don't know the first thing about hygiene. Now we're trying to Destroy the Four Pests. If we go up one and Destroy the Five Pests, we'll be getting rid of you as well!"

At this, Xiwang rolled himself over and sat up proclaiming: "I carried forty loads of water today, you go and try that!"

Shuangshuang replied: "I don't need to. I know how hard that kind of work is. But if I came home after cooking in the canteen, I certainly wouldn't be moaning and groaning like you. *Aiya . . .*"

Washing his face, Xiwang retorted: "It isn't big-talking that tires a person out. These days you seem to think you're above everyone else."

To which Shuangshuang said: "*Ai*, it's not like I'm not busy, work is work! Old Zhao said cooking for the canteen is an important job."

Happy now, Xiwang asked: "Little Chrysanthemum's mother, tell me, just how were my noodles?"

"Delicious. Nice and long and thin," praised Shuangshuang.

Xiwang was delighted at this compliment: "*Hai*, and you haven't even tried any of my specialties yet. If I take those noodles, add a little chicken broth and some shredded chicken, dried shrimps, and seaweed . . . wait till you try that! But right now the canteen doesn't have everything I need. When I used to . . ."

He was just about to continue, but Shuangshuang interrupted: "I don't want to hear about it! I just don't want to hear about it!"

"I didn't finish. How do you know what I was going to say?"

"You think I don't know?" exclaimed Shuangshuang, "You were going to go on about when you were at the Cedar Inn in the North Mountains again."

Xiwang gulped back his spittle: "That's not it at all."

Shuangshuang saw that he was no longer happy and tried to talk him round: "How come you always bring up that Cedar Inn? I just don't want to hear about it. That was the old society, and you were bullied and beaten there. However good the things you made there were, they were all made to serve to landlords, despots, and no-gooders. What did our own families have to eat? Soup so thin you could see your reflection in the bottom of the bowl, rice-husk dumplings so coarse that you couldn't keep them from falling apart. Even at New Year, you'd never see white steamed rolls. Our canteen may provide only simple home cooking right now, but at least it's made for us working people. You don't have to go bragging about that place of yours. I think that if we can continue to Leap Forward like this, then in the future we will harvest bumper crops of grain and raise plenty of pigs and fish. There will certainly come a day when the food from our canteen will be better than it was in that restaurant of yours. Besides all that, do you realize how many pairs of hands you are freeing up with your two hands working in the canteen? I got assigned to the pig farm today. We're only raising 38 pigs right now, but by the end of the year we plan to have 150. Before this, I just had to stay home and wait on you."

Xiwang nodded his head and thought to himself: "What she's saying makes sense." He pondered for a moment and said: "Little Whistle's mother, today I heard someone say that Ma Kesi once talked about getting people to start canteens, have you read that book?"

Shuangshuang replied: "I haven't read that one, but I heard it was En Gesi who said that."

"No," Xiwang insisted, "it was the guy with the surname Ma! . . ."[4]

6

After the wheat harvest, the township became a People's Commune, and Sun Family Village formed a production team.

By this time the Black Hill reservoir had already been completed and the Red Rock River waterway was in operation. A rippling stream of clear water ran by Sun Family Village, converting the surrounding land into paddy fields.

After the move to communes, the masses' enthusiasm was greater than ever, and the forces of the commune flourished. They built a factory complex with hundreds of rooms with red-tiled roofs below the reservoir on Black Mountain and opened up a vegetable oil extractor, a flour mill, a machinery plant, and a cement factory.

---

4. Makesi and Engesi are the Chinese transliterations of the names of Marx and Engels; Xiwang and Shuangshuang have heard the names, but believe them to be Chinese, so we have romanized them as if they were Chinese names, Ma Kesi and En Gesi. Throughout the story Li Zhun pokes affectionate fun at the way his peasant characters grapple with the language of the new age.

The commune established a large husbandry station, a forestry station, and a plant nursery in the hills. To the west of the village, in the area around the Lu Ban temple,[5] they built several thousand pigsties all at once, which was to be the commune's 10,000-animal piggery. Shuangshuang and other women had been looking after pigs for their brigades, and they were brought together to work in the 10,000-animal piggery. With an excellent wheat harvest for the Sun Village Production Team that summer, and the fact that they had been one of the first to start a canteen, there were always people coming through to look around. But with every visit, the Old Party Secretary would give Xiwang a good scolding: the canteen was never very clean, and if they weren't finding flies, they were seeing rats.

Every morning Xiwang and Shuangshuang would leave for work together at the crack of dawn and go home at the end of their shifts when it was dark. When they saw each other, Shuangshuang would always tell Xiwang about the latest happenings at the pig farm, such as one sow giving birth to twenty piglets, new techniques for artificial insemination, and, best of all, Shuangshuang being recognized as a Model Worker when she came up with a more efficient way to feed the pigs: "Fat pigs eat richly, lean pigs eat sparingly; separate them at the trough."

But as for Xiwang, whenever he heard her talk about news from the piggery, he would just sigh and complain: "I can't do this work. Your job's so much better. All I do is get people upset with me!"

Shuangshuang retorted: "What do you mean, upset with you? You don't give anyone special treatment, so what do you have to fear?"

Xiwang said: "What do you know? People get lippy, especially when you are serving them at meal time. All you hear is moaning and complaining."

---

5. Lu Ban is a legendary craftsman and builder of Chinese antiquity.

"I don't believe it," said Shuangshuang, "As long as you're fair to everyone, it doesn't matter if they complain. The only thing you need to worry about is that you're too easily influenced. If someone comes out with a few words of praise, it makes you too big-headed for your hat, and you'll treat them differently!"

Xiwang listened but didn't utter a sound.

That evening, just as Xiwang was making steamed buns, Sun You came over from across the courtyard. Sun You is in his fifties and as his son Jinqiao was the acting canteen superintendent and because the canteen building belonged to his family, he would often come over to the canteen looking at this and touching that, as if afraid someone might damage his property.

Sun You sat off to the side on a small stool, chatting with Xiwang as he watched him take the cover off a steamer basket.

Sun You said: "*Yi*, Xiwang, your steamed buns look great today! The dough is just perfect. You can tell by the color that the flour is good quality."

"That shows you know what you're talking about. These are made from fresh wheat flour." And as Xiwang spoke, he picked up a hot steamed bun: "Here! Try one!"

Sun You got more voluble as he took the bun and ate it: "Xiwang, right now the canteen serves steamed buns only twice a day. As you may already know, a few years ago my family would eat three solid meals after the harvest, and sometimes we would even have an extra snack in the middle of the day!"

Hearing Sun You say this, Xiwang thought to himself: "You may have been able to eat three solid meals a day, but I never could. I think we're doing pretty well for my kids to be able to eat the way they do in the canteen." But a shortcoming of Xiwang's was that often what he felt in his heart was difficult for him to put into words. So instead he pretended to sigh and said, "*Hai*, it's hard to say with things the way they are these days!"

Sun You, seeing how obliging and gullible Xiwang was, came out with a request: "Xiwang, I have something I'd like your help with. Tomorrow is the anniversary of my eldest son's death, and I want to make some sacrificial dishes. It's not really convenient to cook in the house, so I thought I'd have it done in the canteen and take advantage of your culinary expertise."

As Xiwang was accustomed to making only standard fare in the canteen, he thought this might be a good opportunity to show off his skills. And hearing such high praise from Sun You made his head spin. He said: "You just go ahead and bring the stuff over here and leave everything to me. How could I leave you out on a limb?"

That evening Sun You came by. He said he wanted to make five large dishes, but only brought one small chicken. Seeing he only provided one chicken, Xiwang thought to himself: "Now it's you leaving me out on a limb!" But since he had already made him a promise, he had no choice but to make up what was lacking with provisions from the canteen.

It didn't really matter that he was using the basic condiments, but he also had to use up a large basket of the canteen's greens and noodles. Acting Superintendent Jinqiao saw what was happening, but pretended not to notice.

Xiwang cooked for Sun You well into the middle of the night, but didn't have anything to eat himself. When it was all done, there was half a bowl of soup left over. Sun You said: "You go ahead and eat whatever's left."

But Xiwang replied: "Don't you know you don't eat what you cook? I've had enough of the smell and couldn't think of eating it right now."

"Take it home with you then." Sun You urged.

"Nobody eats meat at my house," Xiwang replied. Actually, it wasn't the case that his family didn't eat meat, but that he was afraid of Shuangshuang. He knew Shuangshuang was someone who wouldn't stand for dealings like this. Whenever she entered the canteen, she would repeatedly warn him about it.

But even though Xiwang was very careful, there's no wall that can block the wind completely, and he wasn't able to keep word from getting out. Before two days had gone by, it was the subject for heated discussions among the masses. At first people just speculated about what had transpired. But later someone pasted up a big-character poster in the canteen.

Xiwang was a timid man, and when he saw the big-character poster, he was scared out of his wits. He thought to himself: "When this gets out, there's no way I can avoid getting into trouble. It would be better if I just quit as canteen cook, and then no one will find fault and get angry with me anymore."

Upon returning home, Xiwang saw Shuangshuang and sighed in exasperation.

Shuangshuang ate in the canteen at the pig farm, and didn't know what had happened: "Now what?" she asked.

Xiwang shook his head and said: "It's the canteen, I can't do it anymore."

"What do you mean you can't do it?" asked Shuangshuang. "You're doing well, so how can you not be able to do it anymore? It won't do any good to say you're just afraid of getting into trouble and upsetting people."

Xiwang had originally wanted to say just that, but Shuangshuang beat him to it, and he realized he had to come up with something else. He cleared his throat a couple of times and said: "Little Chrysanthemum's mother, there's something you don't know. I suffer from nausea. It's a sickness I got when I was young and learning to cook. As soon as I got a whiff of steamed buns I'd feel sick. These last few years I've been just fine. Who'd have guessed that once the weather warmed up it would come back? I'm not afraid of hard work. It doesn't matter if I'm out in the fields spreading manure or hoeing, I can do it all. I just dread the smell of steamed buns! As soon as I catch a whiff, I can't eat a thing."

His pitiful words convinced Shuangshuang that he was telling the truth. "Don't get upset," she said. "Have a word with the Old Party Secretary, and see if you can find someone to take over. It's all part of the Great Leap Forward anyway!"

Xiwang picked up his work clothes and said: "You take these over to the Old Party Secretary, and tell him to appoint someone else as quickly as he can. I have to go see the doctor tomorrow."

Shuangshuang didn't realize he was faking, and took his uniform to brigade headquarters. There she bumped into the Old Party Secretary, who was talking to a group that included Fourth Auntie and Guiying. Shuangshuang didn't know what they were talking about and went over to tell them how Xiwang had come down with an illness that made him afraid of the smell of the steamed buns. Before she finished, Guiying and Fourth Auntie, unable to contain themselves, burst out laughing.

"You don't believe it?" asked Shuangshuang, "He really does have this illness!"

The Party Secretary said: "Shuangshuang, that's not his problem. What he's really suffering from is the sickness of not putting Politics in Command! Take a look. This is a big-character poster somebody pasted up." Shuangshuang took the poster from him and read:

> Canteen Cook Sun Xiwang: Two nights ago, Sun You visited the canteen and made up some story about a memorial feast for his elder son. You used provisions from the canteen to make five dishes for him, squandering canteen supplies. If we all act like you, how can our canteen possibly be a success?

When Shuangshuang finished reading the poster, her eyes darkened with anger. She thought to herself: "I told him over and over, but he insisted he'd changed his thinking since the start of the Great Leap Forward. Who knew he was still as stupid as ever!" Upon thinking this, her eyes filled with tears, and her lips were white with fury.

The Old Party Secretary seemed to know what was bothering her and gave her a stool to sit down on and said with a wry smile: "Shuangshuang, there is nothing strange about this. People are just used to doing things the old way. Nowadays we all have to struggle to overcome these old habits. We have to see these wealthy middle peasants clearly for what they are. They're not just out to take advantage of the canteen. From their point of view, the best thing would be for the canteen to collapse. So no matter what kind of work we do now, we have to put Politics in Command."

Shuangshuang asked: "What's 'Politics in Command'?"

The Old Party Secretary replied, "Politics in Command means doing what the Party tells you. No matter what you are doing, you must bear in mind that it is all revolutionary work. It's all work for our Great Leap Forward, working all out for the development of the People's Communes, working so that the masses will enjoy a prosperous life as soon as possible. If in your thinking you are able to understand the Party line, then you will avoid evil, you will not waver, and you will not be deceived by wealthy middle peasants and bad elements!"

Shuangshuang was affected deeply by what the Old Party Secretary said. She had thought that while Xiwang was in the canteen, as long as he did not steal and behaved fairly and honestly, then all would be well. She'd never thought it was also necessary to have Politics in Command.

The Old Party Secretary continued: "If Xiwang doesn't want to do it any more then so be it. He's really too weak-willed. It's just that we can't find a suitable person to take over. The canteen is very important. This summer we'll be cultivating several thousand *mu*[6]

---

6. *Mu*: an area of land equivalent to one-sixth of an acre or one-fifteenth of a hectare.

of paddy rice. We need to flood the fields several times a month, and we want to get a bumper harvest. If the canteen isn't run properly, we won't be able to do it."

Listening to the Old Party Secretary, Shuangshuang got quite excited: "Party Secretary, how about I go and cook in the canteen? When we were originally planning for the canteen, I wanted to be the cook, but at the time everybody said it was Xiwang who had the skills. Now I'm prepared to do it! I promise I'll put Politics in Command!"

Shuangshuang had hardly finished when Guiying shouted out: "Actually we'd all thought of you for the job! Now we'll all clap our hands and welcome you!"

Fourth Auntie added excitedly: "Shuangshuang can do it! She won't be like that spineless Xiwang!"

"All right," said the Old Party Secretary. "You can go. I'll have a word with the people at the piggery, they've just had some Youth Leaguers assigned to work there." He then pointed to the uniform in Shuangshuang's hands: "What's that?"

Shuangshuang blushed: "It's a uniform! Xiwang's asked me to deliver it to you for him!"

Guiying interrupted: "Let's go! This job's going to be staying in your family anyway!" When she finished speaking, she and Fourth Auntie took Shuangshuang by the arms and marched her off toward the canteen.

Xiwang was at home, *suona* in hand, playing along with the tune being broadcast over the local radio network. He was playing with gusto when Shuangshuang entered the room. Seeing Shuangshuang had returned home, he quickly put down the *suona*. Shuangshuang angrily tossed the uniform on the bed. Xiwang hastily asked: "Why did you bring that back?"

"Just you tell me what you're suffering from!" she demanded.

"I'm afraid of the steam from making the buns!"

Shuangshuang glared at him: "Nonsense! How could you have let yourself get fooled by that wealthy middle peasant Sun You? Tell me!"

Xiwang saw that his cover was blown and clammed up.

Shuangshuang spelled out what it was he had done: "What am I always telling you, and yet you still get yourself into something like this! You've forgotten what kind of lives we used to live. Now the Party is leading us into the Great Leap Forward and establishing the People's Communes so that we can have a good life as soon as possible. Not only must we obey the Party and obey Chairman Mao, but we also must love the Party and stand up for everything it proposes. We must struggle against those who try to sabotage it! But what does it mean when you do something like that!"

Shuangshuang went on to tell Xiwang what the Old Party Secretary had said, and the incident of someone putting up a big-character poster to reveal what happened at the canteen. Xiwang hung his head in shame and didn't respond. Finally he spoke: "Little Chrysanthemum's mother, it all happened because I wasn't thinking straight. What do you think I should do now? Could you write another big-character poster for me making my self-criticism?"

Shuangshuang said: "If you want one written, write it yourself! Just write down what you just said."

"So do I still have to go to the canteen tomorrow?" Xiwang asked.

"You don't need to," Shuangshuang said. "The Old Party Secretary says you didn't put Politics in Command, so you're not allowed back to the canteen. I've got this uniform now, I'll be going to the canteen as a cook."

Xiwang was shocked: "So you're going to be taking over my job?"

Shuangshuang said: "I'm certainly not going to be like you!"

Xiwang nodded: "I believe that. But what am I going to do? Maybe I should go to the piggery."

Shuangshuang said: "At the piggery it's still Politics in Command!"

Xiwang said: "You have to take the long view. A seventeen-year-old can still live another seventeen years, and an eighteen-year-old another eighteen, we can all get more mature. Maybe a rat's tail never changes, but I'm not a rat's tail and I can change!"

Xiwang was pleading, and Shuangshuang had to chuckle. "Go on and write your big-character poster," she said.

7

Right from the first day Shuangshuang went to the canteen, it was clear that things were going to be different. That morning at breakfast Sun You was out of sorts because he had been criticized for the cooking incident; he stood to one side and made a show of pounding his chest: "*Ai*! To be a cook you've really got to put your heart here!"

"I don't need to," Shuangshuang replied, "mine's always been there. Whoever thinks they can take advantage of the canteen has got another thing coming!"

Shuangshuang's response was sharp and to the point. Delighted, the commune members exclaimed: "This time everything is going to be fine, we've finally got someone in the canteen who's really principled."

Later that morning Shuangshuang gathered the cooks together: "This canteen of ours needs a thorough cleaning! What do you say we clean up all the piles of bricks and tiles in the courtyard and whitewash the walls?" Several of the cooks felt this was a great idea, except for Jinqiao, who said: "The team is so busy now! Where are we going to find the help?"

"We don't need anyone else from the team," Shuangshuang replied, "We'll make food by day and turn ourselves into shock troops by night. A few evenings of work by the shock troops ought to see it done."

"But I have to do the accounting at night," said Jinqiao.

"You get on with that," Shuangshuang quickly replied. "Leave this to us. What is there to fear in a few nights without sleep!"

Guiying added: "I don't mind working nights. They're forming shock troops in the team right now as well, aren't they?

Jinqiao saw that everyone was determined and had no choice but to agree. He said: "These bricks and tiles were piled up here by my dad. We were planning to use them to make foundations if we did any more building in the future. If you're cleaning up, you can move them over to our north compound."

Shuangshuang said: "Okay, just tell us where to move them."

That night, after the women had finished washing the dishes and putting the kitchen in order, they took advantage of the fact it was a moonlit night, picked up some large bamboo baskets and began the task of cleaning up. The first night, they worked right through to cockcrow and cleared away all the piles of bricks. The second, Shuangshuang brought over two carrying-pole loads of lime from the commune factory and a couple of cracked pots. She made up some brushes from scraps of hemp, and together with Guiying and some others, she began to whitewash the walls from top to bottom. They worked for two nights straight, until the walls of the canteen courtyard gleamed like white marble.

Once the courtyard was tidied up, they took out all the cooking utensils and gave them a thorough cleaning. The cutting board, steamer baskets, pots, bowls, ladles, and spoons were scrubbed until they sparkled and not a fleck of dust could be seen. The Old Party Secretary was ecstatic when he came by to take a look: "This just shows that with a little hard work anything can be accomplished. You've all struggled hard the last few days and turned the canteen around in no time."

Shuangshuang said: "We want to do our best to be a canteen with Four Pests Eliminated in the next evaluation. We guarantee there won't be a single fly or rat in here. We need to ask you for some cloth to make covers for the cutting board, pots, and water vats."

The Old Party Secretary said: "We can do this. You really need to achieve Four Pests Eliminated status. Let's avoid what happened last time there was an inspection, when a great big rat ran out from that *kang* brick stove over there."

"You mean that one in the corner over there?" Shuangshuang asked, pointing to an old beaten-earth *kang* piled high with tiles and jars.

"That's the one all right," said the Old Party Secretary.

"Don't you worry," Shuangshuang said. "We'll wage a campaign against it tonight and dig it out!"

That night Shuangshuang, Guiying, Fourth Auntie, and a few others started digging out the old *kang*. Over the past few days, while the rest of them had been cleaning, Jinqiao had just stayed in his room fiddling with his abacus and offering no help at all. But that night, when he heard people digging out the *kang*, he suddenly seemed to get alarmed about something and came scurrying out. The minute he entered the kitchen he demanded: "What are you digging for?"

"We're digging out a rat hole, there's a big rat in here!" Shuangshuang said as she shoveled dirt out.

"There can't be a rat in here!" Jinqiao said. "Stop digging."

The women weren't going to listen to him and just concentrated on digging down deeper. Jinqiao, seeing them dig even harder, went over and pried the pickax from Guiying's hands: "Get over there, let me do it! You women don't have the strength for it."

Jinqiao then grabbed the pickax and scraped around at the sides of the hole rather than digging any deeper into it. It was as though there was something hidden in that old *kang*. Shuangshuang asked: "Jinqiao, what are you doing just scratching at it, are you afraid of scaring the rat?"

Jinqiao asked: "How can there possibly be a rat in here?"

"Get over here!" Shuangshuang ordered, and started digging in deeper. But the more dirt Shuangshuang scraped out the more Jinqiao pushed back in, provoking her to swing the pickax with even more determination. There was a clanging sound, and her hands went numb—her pickax had struck something hard!

"What was that?" Shuangshuang and Guiying cried out in unison.

Jinqiao's forehead broke out in a sweat: "It was nothing, probably just a tile."

But by then Shuangshuang had realized something fishy was going on, and she yelled out: "It doesn't matter if it's a ghost or a monster. We're Eliminating the Four Pests. We have to do away with it!" With this, she went straight back to digging at the *kang*. Once they had broken open the top of the *kang*, they dug out a Liberation-model water pump.

After they had dug out the water pump, Jinqiao's face went pale. The water pump, which had been buried for a couple of years, had been hidden by his family when they entered the cooperative. When the canteen was located in his family's courtyard, it all happened so quickly they didn't have time to move it elsewhere.

Shuangshuang asked: "Jinqiao, how is it possible that your family has a water pump buried inside this *kang*?"

Jinqiao said: "I really don't know. My dad knows a lot of people . . . or maybe one of our relatives put it here."

Shuangshuang realized she wasn't going to get any reasonable explanation from him. She looked at the clock on the table, and as it was already four o'clock she suggested: "Let's not worry about who it belongs to. How about we just leave it here overnight and report it to the brigade tomorrow morning? It's late, everybody go home and get some sleep!" And with that they all went their separate ways.

When she got home, Shuangshuang heard that Xiwang was sound asleep and snoring. She didn't want to wake him, and so didn't dare light the lamp. She just slumped down fully dressed at the edge of the bed and went to sleep. Almost immediately, she heard a voice whispering outside the window: "Xiwang! Xiwang!"

Listening carefully, Shuangshuang recognized it was the voice of Sun You. She listened but didn't make a sound.

After Sun You had been calling him for a while, Xiwang woke up: "Who's there?"

From outside, Sun You said: "It's me. Xiwang, I need to talk to you about something important!"

Xiwang got out of bed grumbling to himself. He went out into the courtyard and opened the main gate. Shuangshuang could hear Sun You's voice mumbling on for ages, but she couldn't make out what he was saying. Then she heard Xiwang exclaim: "No way! It's Politics in Command for me from now on! I can't do that for you!"

Sun You pleaded: "Look, Xiwang, we are both members of the Sun clan, we have to stick together. If this gets out, I'll be disgraced. It's like this . . ." He murmured on inaudibly for a while, and then Xiwang responded: "What do you mean by 'in the future our two families can use it together'? You still believe in private ownership! I think you'd better hurry up and get rid of that way of thinking. I'm telling you, the two of us are not on the same path. Get out of here! You should know it doesn't pay to annoy Li Shuangshuang!"

"Don't say anything about it then. I'll just hand it over myself." With this, Sun You scuttled off.

Listening to Xiwang from inside the room Shuangshuang almost burst out laughing. But she hadn't been able to hear what Sun You had said, and so after Xiwang returned to the room she opened her eyes and asked: "Who was that just now?"

"Old Sun You," Xiwang replied.

Shuangshuang asked: "What did he want with you?"

Xiwang shuffled uncomfortably: "It doesn't matter, I sent him away. Now get some sleep!" As far as Xiwang was concerned, now that Sun You was gone it was all over, as long as he didn't follow him down the wrong path.

But Shuangshuang sat up and said: "What exactly was that all about?"

Xiwang tried to keep quiet, but he couldn't withstand Shuang-shuang's interrogation and had to tell her: "When Sun You came by just now he tried to convince me that as long as you don't say anything about that water pump you dug out, then the others will keep quiet too. And that in the future, when he gets to use the water pump, he'll share it with us. . . ." He had not yet finished speaking when Shuangshuang threw off the quilt and jumped down from the bed: "So that old guy still wants to stick to the old ways!" And she headed outside.

Xiwang quickly asked: "Just where are you going?"

"To look for him!" Shuangshuang said as she buttoned up her jacket and stormed out.

As Xiwang watched her leave the room, he sighed to himself, "*Ai!* It's true what they say, that oil and water don't mix. Where he's concerned, she's got a shorter fuse than a firecracker!"

Shuangshuang went to Sun You's home but couldn't find him there, so she ran straight to brigade headquarters to look for the Old Party Secretary. It was still dark, and the Old Party Secretary and some committee members had just retuned from inspecting the paddy fields. They were furious when they heard her account of the events.

"When he joined the cooperative the year before last, he said he'd sold his water pump. But he's been hiding it all along!" said Yushun.

"Now we've found somebody we can make an example of," the Old Party Secretary pointed out. "Often when we talk about people who stick to the old ways, some of the masses don't believe us. Now we can really get the masses talking about this and make them see what kind of tendencies these wealthy middle peasants are harboring. And as for Jinqiao, it doesn't matter that he's still young. His mind is full of selfish thoughts. If you've got someone suitable to replace him, do it right away."

That very night, a mass meeting took place in the courtyard of the canteen of the Sun Village Brigade. At the meeting Shuangshuang and Xiwang reported on how Sun You selfishly hid the water pump and tried to corrupt Xiwang. The masses argued heatedly with Sun You, and they wouldn't let up until they forced him to confess his plans for following the old path of capitalism and made him promise that he would go along with everyone else in future.

8

After being tested in several political campaigns, Shuangshuang was admitted into the Communist Party. After entering the Party, Shuangshuang was even more enthusiastic and responsible, and the Sun Village public canteen was managed to the even greater satisfaction of the masses.

After some persuasion, Sun You offered to contribute his water pump to the commune for an agreed price. This came at a time when the County Party Committee was calling for extensive mechanization of canteen cooking facilities, and the brigade issued the water pump to the canteen. When Shuangshuang, Guiying, and the others got hold of the water pump, they set to work on the task of mechanization.

First they installed the water pump at the well, and then they rigged up two water pipes, with taps directly over the main cooking pot and the water vat, so that there was running water for drinking and other uses. A man called Yang had been appointed to the canteen specifically to carry water after Xiwang left, and now Yang could be spared to assist at the piggery.

Now that the women had successfully upgraded their cooking equipment, they became bolder than ever.

At first the commune machine shop had helped them out with a machine to flatten the dough for noodles. Later the machine shop got too busy, so Shuangshuang said: "Come on! Let's do things ourselves! There's nothing human beings can't do. It's just a matter of liberating our thinking!" They borrowed a set of tools from a carpenter, found some pieces of wood, and worked at it all night. First they made a machine to chop vegetables, then another to rinse rice. Then, after Shuangshuang had visited the commune hospital, she discovered that the insulated containers they had for keeping food hot worked very effectively, and following the design of the people at the hospital, she designed a couple of food-delivery carts that automatically kept food warm. Within a couple of weeks, they had managed to bring about a complete mechanization of the cooking system, using local resources.

After the Spring Festival, there was a major countywide inspection to evaluate canteens. Sun Family Village canteen was judged to be one of the First-class Red Flag Canteens for the county. The County Committee also proposed providing a greater variety of food, under the slogan of letting commune members "Eat Well, Eat Enough, Eat Flavorfully." In her efforts to carry out this directive, Shuangshuang had another row with Jinqiao.

It was now the first month of the lunar year, and the commune was preparing for the first major irrigation of the wheat fields that year. Because the Production Team harvested so many sweet potatoes the year before, flour made from sweet potatoes constituted a third of everyone's diet. Sweet-potato flour is something people get tired of if it's not properly prepared. Shuangshuang noticed that the commune members all enjoyed their steamed buns at lunch and noodles at dinner, but of the three large pots of sweet-potato porridge served at breakfast, there was always half a pot left over. She said to Jinqiao: "Jinqiao, we have to find a way to get more variety. If we can vary the way we serve things made with sweet-potato flour, the commune members will certainly be happy eating them. For example, we could make pancakes or noodles . . ."

Before she'd finished speaking, Jinqiao sneered: "Sweet potatoes are always going to be sweet potatoes. Are you going to be able to turn them into flowers?"

Shuangshuang said: "Don't be so sure! Last night we did an experiment and came up with a Great Leap noodle: we mixed in sweet-potato flour and white flour fifty-fifty, and the finished product is even tastier than regular noodles made with white flour!"

Jinqiao said: "I never heard of anyone inventing noodles! This is a big enterprise with several hundred people eating. It's not just your family and your little coal stove."

Shuangshuang retorted angrily: "Our plan is precisely to make it work in the canteen! Haven't you seen the half pot of sweet-potato porridge that gets left over every morning?"

Jinqiao said: "As far as I'm concerned, that means they've got too much to eat. They'd have had to eat that food if it had been a few years ago, wouldn't they? Now the whole family can eat their fill together, but they're so picky!"

Shuangshuang could see an ulterior motive in what he was saying, and she immediately got annoyed with him: "Jinqiao, what are you trying to say? That was then, and this is now, we have to make sure the commune members eat well!"

"I'm not saying we let them starve!" shouted Jinqiao.

"But you're not trying to do a good job of running the canteen," said Shuangshuang, "You're just a Retrogressionist!"

The two of them were about to get into a major argument when Xiwang happened to come by to pick up their slops for the piggery.

He saw Shuangshuang grabbing hold of Jinqiao and shouting: "Come on! Let's go to brigade headquarters and find the Old Party Secretary!"

Jinqiao was waving his hand in refusal, yelling: "I'm not going!" and pushing Shuangshuang aside.

This really incensed Xiwang; he strode over and confronted Jinqiao: "What's on your mind? Don't you like Li Shuangshuang's ideas? Let me tell you something! I'll speak plainly here: you may have moved your body to Cao Cao's camp, but your heart still sides with the Han army.[7] Your mind still hasn't got round to the idea of making a success of the canteen!"

At this point the masses all gathered around, and everyone was really angry. There was some heated debate, and Jinqiao was criticized for his unreasonableness. Just as everyone was talking, the Old Party Secretary arrived. After he found out the cause of the argument, his face went red with fury. In a steady voice, he demanded of Jinqiao: "What was wrong with Shuangshuang's suggestion? The leadership has called several meetings to urge people to find ways of giving food more variety; what have *you* done about it?"

Jinqiao pursed his lips and remained silent, but the Old Party Secretary pointed at him and continued: "For a fellow as young as you are, you have a very reactionary way of looking at things! You haven't changed at all!" Then he said to Shuangshuang: "Shuangshuang, those experiments you did that came up with the Great Leap noodles and pancakes, they were a success, and we've reported the good news to the County Party Committee. This is great!"

Everyone burst into applause.

When Shuangshuang got home after dinner, Xiwang was concerned: "What about Jinqiao?"

Shuangshuang replied: "Still at the canteen. I hear the Party Committee is going to investigate his work."

---

7. A reference to the classic novel *Sanguo* (Three kingdoms), which is set after the fall of the Han dynasty in the third century. Cao Cao, ruler of the kingdom of Wei, is the enemy of Liu Bei, commander of the remaining forces of the Han.

Xiwang said: "Shuangshuang, I'm a bit worried about you. He's had a bit of education, and he's a cadre. He's the superintendent and you're a cook. If we've got on the wrong side of him today and can't resolve it, in future . . ."

"There you go again!" Shuangshuang laughed. "The Party's in charge now! As long as our standpoint and our actions are correct, if I've got the right on my side, I'll go anywhere I choose. What is there to fear? We're acting for the masses, for the commune and for the Great Leap. If he tries to hold me back, it's not going to work. However retrogressionist he is, I'll keep fighting him!"

Xiwang said: "It's all very well to say that, but how can we know how the higher-ups are going to investigate it?"

Shuangshuang said: "Don't you worry about him! I'm grown up now, and he's not going to bully me anymore! Anyway, I have something I need to come to you to ask you for instruction, as my teacher."

Xiwang said: "Actually I have something I need some instruction with as well."

Shuangshuang said: "You first. What's up?"

Xiwang said: "At the piggery we're being called on to set up something called a 'pig dossier.' You're always writing and drawing, and making calculations, but I wasn't very serious about going to the community school. So this dossier really has me stumped."

Shuangshuang said: "This dossier is probably a record for each pig from birth, with its temperament, weight, and what illnesses it's had."

Xiwang said: "You're right! That's it!"

Shuangshuang said: "That's straightforward enough. I'll have a look at it for you. But you have to learn some new skills too!"

Xiwang interjected: "I have my own inventions too! You should go and see how fat those few dozen pigs of mine are!"

"That's fine!" said Shuangshuang. "Today we have to do some research on Great Leap noodles. What do you think? If we mix in sweet-potato flour fifty-fifty, how are we going to get the noodles long and thin?"

Xiwang said: "*Hai*! Just put a little extra salt in the water you cook them in! Let's go! I'll head over there with you."

Xiwang went to the canteen with Shuangshuang, and after a night working on it, they finally succeeded with their noodle experiment. In addition to that, in order to prepare the pancakes faster and in greater quantities, Shuangshuang came up with a new pancake stove with cooking surfaces at different levels and six air vents. The main thing about this stove was that it saved manpower and fuel, and one person could fry 400 pancakes in an hour.

Next morning the team had people out in the fields in a shock troop watering the wheat shoots to combat spring drought, and the youngsters were also out in the fields spreading ash and nightsoil on the fields.

Shuangshuang, Guiying, and Fourth Auntie got the noodles made and fried up 400 pancakes. They loaded them up in the insulated cart, which Shuangshuang pushed, and headed off to the 10,000 *mu* high-yield plot by the piggery to deliver lunch.

It was now into the second month of the lunar calendar, and the peach orchard the brigade had planted outside the village was blossoming a brilliant pink, which from a distance looked like clouds on the horizon at dawn. Willow saplings lined both sides of the road, their fronds swaying gently in the wind like golden threads, sending willow floss dancing through the air.

In the high-yield wheat fields, beneath her feet all she could hear was the gurgling sound of running water. The cheerful sound of laughter echoed across the surface of the water. It had only been two days since Shuangshuang's last visit to the high-yield plot, yet she found that the glossy green wheat seedlings had already grown thick and sturdy as they brushed against her knees.

She pushed the meal cart over to a water-pump platform

beneath a large willow tree and waved a handkerchief as she called everyone over. Laughing and chatting, they gathered around her.

A young man asked: "Auntie Shuangshuang, what did you make for us today? I heard you have something new."

Laughing, Shuangshuang replied: "Everyone, open it up and have a look, then you'll know. And be sure to tell me what you think!"

"With Li Shuangshuang's cooking, it doesn't matter what it is," an old man added. "It's always so clean, you can eat it with your eyes closed and have nothing to worry about."

After Shuangshuang had called everyone over, she went over to turn the water pump in order to keep the water flowing. A young girl called out to her: "Auntie Shuangshuang, come over and eat with us, you need to take a break as well."

"I'll eat when I go back," Shuangshuang replied.

An old man standing beside them said: "*Ai*, don't bother about her. She's used to it. Whenever she comes here with the food, she's not happy if she's not working that wheel for a while."

While Shuangshuang worked the waterwheel, they all ate. After the food cart was opened, all she could hear was the din of their excitement.

One person said: "What kind of noodles are these? They're like vermicelli!"

"Try them, they're so fine, they're better than flour noodles."

"You'd never be able to tell these are sweet-potato noodles!"

Another young man yelled out: "Look, there are also hot pancakes! C'mon! Crispy on the outside and soft on the inside, they're called 'Old Man's Delight'!"

"Auntie Shuangshuang! The canteen has launched a sputnik! We're going to put up a big-character poster about you!"

As she listened from the well platform to everyone eating and talking amongst themselves, Shuangshuang stood back and smiled.

Turning the water pump, she watched the crystal-clear spring water gushing along the channel toward the fields, and she listened to the slurping sounds of people eating fragrant, sweet, delicious food.

It was just then she suddenly realized that the beads of sweat that poured off the canteen workers were flowing along with the spring water into the rich, flourishing high-yield fields, turning into wheat and rice.

After the meal was over, Shuangshuang pushed her cart back toward the village. When she got close to the commune's 10,000-animal piggery, she suddenly heard the familiar sounds of a *suona* playing.

She walked by the wall around the piggery to take a look and saw Xiwang sitting on a tree stump by the pigsties playing his *suona*. He played one tune, and a group of piglets trotted over to the trough in an orderly fashion and started to eat. He played another tune, and a herd of feeder pigs went off from beside the trough into an area of the yard, squealing as they ran.

Shuangshuang watched in amazement, thinking to herself: "Who'd have thought he'd have that kind of knack?" Then she turned and went in.

Xiwang smiled as he saw Shuangshuang coming in: "You're coming to watch me at work. See how I feed the pigs: those are the piglets, those are the feeder pigs, and those are the porkers. Do you think they're fat enough?" He pointed to groups of pigs of different sizes as he spoke.

Shuangshuang laughed: "You've really come up with some new ideas! Do they all understand it when you play them their tunes?"

"Sure they do!" said Xiwang, "They do whatever my *suona* tells them to. The big ones put on three pounds a day!" Then he added softly: "How's it going with Jinqiao?"

Just as Shuangshuang was about to answer, the radio at the piggery began to broadcast: "Good news everyone! Sun Family Village's canteen has invented a kind of Great Leap noodles and a multilevel pancake stove. Today the commune is holding a meeting there, and inviting other canteens to send representatives over to inspect it. Also, the Commune Committee has decided that Li Shuangshuang will take over as canteen superintendent. She has already been selected as a Top-level Model Worker for our whole county, and on the tenth of this month she will attend a congress of labor heroes!"

After the broadcast ended, Xiwang was so moved his eyes filled with tears: "Shuangshuang! Shuangshuang! The Party truly has vision!"

A crowd of girls came running out of the piggery toward them, laughing and shouting. Shuangshuang said: "I hope you will work hard looking after the pigs. Maybe next year we'll go to Beijing together."

Xiwang said: "I'll certainly try to keep up with you!"

Translated by Johanna Hood and Robert Mackie with Richard King

THE STORY OF THE CRIMINAL LI TONGZHONG

by Zhang Yigong

1. Qingming Festival, 1979

Why does it always have to rain at Qingming?[1] Fine strands of silent rain wove themselves into a silver net, enmeshing the thoughts that swirled in the mind of the District Party Secretary Tian Zhenshan.

Tian Zhenshan was riding in a jeep, traveling to a remote county in the mountains to attend a ceremony that would restore the good name of a Party branch secretary.

This Party branch secretary was a man who had left the human world nineteen years before. Over the course of those nineteen

---

Drafted April 1979, revised August 1979; published in the January 1980 issue of the journal *Shouhuo* (Harvest).

1. The Qingming Festival, which falls in the first week of April every year, is the day for visiting and tidying graves and remembering the dead.

years, history had brought unimaginable turmoil and played who knows how many terrible tricks! But throughout that time, Tian Zhenshan had never forgotten this man, Li Tongzhong, born in the flight from famine, indentured as a shepherd for the local land-lord the year he turned ten, local militia chief at the time of Land Reform, Korean War volunteer, demobilized disabled veteran, Li Family Stockade Brigade's "peg-legged Party secretary" Li Tong-zhong. This was the Li Tongzhong who had ended his life as Li Tongzhong "the Criminal Ringleader, guilty of colluding with the Hillside Inn Grain Station manager, inciting the unwitting masses, and plundering a state granary."

Now history had come to a new verdict: Li Tongzhong had committed no crime. Though there had been fierce conflict in the County and District Party Committees over the rehabilitation of Li Tongzhong, and though there had been some comrades who were still uncomfortable with the decision, the newly appointed district Party secretary had decided to attend the rehabilitation ceremony. In order to make the living wiser, in order to straighten out the affairs of the world, he wanted to go to the little mountain hamlet he had left nineteen years before to free a shackled ghost from his chains.

The jeep jolted as it sped up the mountain road. Tian Zhong-shan opened the window and let the fresh mountain breeze blow the silent drizzle onto the deep wrinkles that lined his face. He closed his eyes and thought back to the extraordinary events that had unfolded nineteen years before. . . .

2. The spring famine

It was in the spring of the year 1960 that Party Branch Secretary Li Tongzhong became the Criminal Plunderer Li Tongzhong.

When that accursed spring came to Li Family Stockade, it brought with it a famine the like of which had seldom been seen.

Since the first day of spring, when the last pot of corn mush had been mixed with ten buckets of water in the great communal cooking vat, the 490-odd men, women, and children of Li Family Stockade had had nothing to eat but a thin gruel of sweet potatoes. At noon the "Master of the Three Halls" Uncle Gang, canteen superintendent for the three production teams, squatted in the corner of a storeroom bereft of rice and flour and secretly began to cry: "God in heaven! *Ai, ai, ai, ai* . . . open your eyes, . . . you can't be making us pick up the begging bowls again, *ai ai ai . . .*"

Crying, too, is a contagion. The sound of Uncle Gang's crying slipped out through a crack in the door that wasn't sealed tight enough; first it infected the old women who had come to the canteen bearing food bowls to be filled with gruel, then it spread to young wives whose children were complaining of hunger, and later it became a plague that even the men had no power to resist.

"Don't cry. You mustn't cry." Li Tongzhong hurried over from the brigade office, his heavy artificial leg crunching in the snow, to explain to everyone why they weren't to cry: "If you cry too much, your eyes will be sore and your heads will spin. If you cry too much, you'll harm your health. I'm just off to check at commune headquarters again. Maybe there will be news of a grain allocation!"

The crying died down. Wordlessly, everyone stared at the Party secretary. This remarkably robust young man was himself showing the strains of hunger. His eyelids were so swollen it looked as if you could squeeze water out of them, and his cheeks were sunken into his square face. But when he set off out of the village on his seven-and-a-half-pound artificial leg, he thrust the willow staff his wife Zhang Cuiying had given him a good distance ahead; his five feet four-and-a-half-inch frame was as upright as ever in its faded army uniform, and his dark bloodshot eyes still gleamed. His posture and his expression told them all: there were still a few battles left in this military veteran.

But Li Tongzhong's heart was heavy. He was discouraged and resentful at the prospect of begging for food from "Hot-shot Secretary" Yang Wenxiu.

The Hot-shot Secretary was an exceptional literary talent and had been an elementary school teacher. Later he was promoted to a job with the Propaganda Office of the County Party Committee. He slaved away at this for five years and gradually came to the realization that someone like him, with no experience at the regional or township level, would never get any further in his career than writing Party documents to order. He was trapped in a confined space, like dough rising inside an eggshell. So in 1958 he volunteered enthusiastically to be sent to work at the grassroots level and was appointed Party secretary at Ten-mile Store People's Commune. From that point on, he had dedicated all his efforts to anticipating the wishes of his superiors and providing them, within a couple of days, with exemplary models appropriate to whatever it was they had in mind. For example, he had heard even before he went to Ten-mile Store of a debate among Party theoreticians as to whether one country could achieve communism in advance of the rest of the world, and it immediately occurred to him that this was the same kind of thinking as Lenin's proposal that socialist revolution might first be victorious in one country or a group of countries. Extrapolating from this, he came up with the theory that it would be entirely feasible for one *commune* to be the first to achieve communism. And this commune would, of course, be Ten-mile Store. Therefore, on the day after he took office, he announced to everyone that Ten-mile Store Commune would enter communism in two years. From that point on, he smoked two packs of cigarettes every day, and his eyes, so narrow that they looked as if they had been cut into his face with a knife, were forever squinting, blinking, flashing with a mystical gleam, as he figured out ways to make Ten-mile Store stay out in front in all respects, selecting times when County Party Secretary Tian Zhenshan was not away on business to announce each item of good news to the County Party Committee.

At times of overexertion, actions can easily become distorted. The designs of his superiors—regardless of whether they made sense or not—would be extravagantly embellished once Yang Wenxiu got to work on them. During the campaign to produce iron and steel, he ordered all villages and production teams to smash cooking utensils for smelting into iron and to confiscate every metal object they could lay their hands on. Not a single door stud or door knocker was spared, and all were tipped into the numerous rustic furnaces. Li Tongzhong's wife was in a panic and prayed the whole day that they would not be ordered to smelt copper, since her husband's name Tongzhong meant "Copper Bell." When the County Party Committee called for the cultivation of High-yield Experimental Plots, Yang Wenxiu added an extra instruction to the teams: these high-yield plots were to be set up by the side of the road, to create the best possible impression. In order to manifest the dynamic spirit quoted in the papers, with "Old men surpassing the fierce Huang Zhong, young wives outclassing the woman warrior Mu Guiying,"[2] he had the commune members working the plots in costume; to a mighty din of drums and gongs, the old men went to the fields sporting long beards borrowed from the amateur operatic group, the women in medieval theatrical dress, brandishing banners like Mu Guiying's inscribed with the word "General."

Li Tongzhong watched all this sadly. He felt that the new commune Party secretary was putting on a show all day, a show aimed at his superiors, with the hope of winning their admiration and praise. He urged the cadres of Li Family Stockade: "We're all farmers here

---

2. Huang Zhong was an army commander from the Three Kingdoms period in the third century; for Mu Guiying, see note 2 to *Li Shuangshuang* above.

in Li Family Stockade, not actors; we don't want to be fooling around with stage gestures and fake weapons."

But Li Family Stockade wasn't able to escape the misfortune that accompanied the Hot-shot Party Secretary. The previous year had been dry, and the year before that the Iron and Steel Battalion hadn't come back from their work in the mountains in time for planting wheat, so the summer plantings had gone in late, and the shoots had been sparse. Then in autumn there had been a "choking drought," so neither the summer nor the autumn weather was as favorable as in the previous years. But the Hot-shot Party Secretary had led the way with the bold slogan "In Years without Rain, Three Things Won't Change," those three things being that production wouldn't change, the amount provided to the state wouldn't change, and allocations to commune members wouldn't change. The result was that two of the things that weren't going to change fell by the wayside, and it was only by enforcing the policy against concealing production that the middle one was made to come about. And it was precisely because their payment to the state didn't change that, in the very year that Ten-mile Store Commune was supposed to be entering communism, Li Tongzhong was obliged to hobble to the commune headquarters again and again to make reports to Yang Wenxiu about a spring famine that made the prospect of communism seem more than somewhat uncertain.

Every trip to the commune was a sore test of Li Tongzhong's patience. The first occasion came at a time when the commune members of Li Family Stockade were still able to eat two ounces of grain per day, and it also came as Yang Wenxiu was hanging up on the wall a certificate of commendation awarded to him by the County Party Committee and the County Management Committee for fulfilling his duties in requisitioning grain above and beyond the set quota.

"Comrade Li Tongzhong." Yang Wenxiu's voice was stern. "Do you know what kind of people they are that are complaining about a problem with grain?"

"Yes, I do."

"Who are they?"

"The poor and lower-middle peasants."

"What's that?" Yang Wenxiu was momentarily nonplussed, his cigarette poised awkwardly in mid-air, but he quickly recovered and brought it back round: "That's the *new* middle peasants, it must be the *new*, *upper*-middle peasants, comrade. You shouldn't be sitting on a bench with wealthy peasants."

Without waiting for a reply from Li Tongzhong, the Hot-shot Party Secretary hurried out of the office with Great Leaping strides.

The second occasion was when Li Family Stockade was on the verge of running out of grain, and it was also when Yang Wenxiu saw with his own eyes that the elm trees of Li Family Stockade had been stripped of their bark for food.

"Li Family Stockade's grain *is* a little tight." Yang Wenxiu avoided Li Tongzhong's eyes, which had dark heavy bags under them. "But the spirit of the moment is still Opposing Rightism, opposing those who look up to their superiors with hands outstretched. It's not that I mind asking the county for some grain, I'm just concerned that the Rightist hat would not be a comfortable one to wear!"

"Then you can give the hat to me." Li Tongzhong said dourly. "If opposing Rightism can produce some grain, or get us anything to eat, then I'm prepared to wear the Rightist hat for the next ten thousand years."

"Comrade, you mustn't let your emotions get the better of you." Yang Wenxiu was pacing back and forth. "It's not only Li Family Stockade that is short of grain. I've heard that the District Party Committee is having a meeting right now to talk about protecting the people and preserving the livestock, and Secretary Tian from the county is taking part. When he gets back we can find out about the spirit of the meeting and then decide what to do. Your canteen vegetable plots look okay. Just hold out a bit longer."

Li Tongzhong, you have a remarkable capacity for endurance! But history proves that there are limits to how much the stomach can bear. After three days of turnip gruel, there were sounds of weeping from the commune members at the door of the public canteen. Three days earlier Li Tongzhong had sent someone to County Party Secretary Tian Zhenshan with an Emergency Report; at the suggestion of Li Family Stockade's resident scholar, the accountant Cui Wen, he had inscribed three explosive exclamation marks at the end. As yet, however, there had been no reply. Li Tongzhong had to hobble back again, his artificial leg clattering on the black stone steps up to the commune office.

"Tongzhong, you don't need to say anything." Yang Wenxiu was pushing his bike out to the gate. "Secretary Tian is back, the County Committee has given notice of a special meeting to discuss the living conditions of the commune members. Why don't you just go home and wait?"

"But what are we going to do right now?"

Yang Wenxiu was already on his bike and pedaling like the wind. He turned back and yelled: "Turnips."

Li Tongzhong went back. As he was walking up Hero Slope, he felt dizzy, lost his footing, and tumbled into a ditch. He lay motionless in a snowdrift, too weak to pull himself up. He really wanted to just to lie there like that, lie down forever and never get up again. But then he thought of the hundreds of people waiting for him and remembered the meeting that was going on at the County Committee. Perhaps Secretary Tian had already received his Emergency Report. He swallowed a few mouthfuls of snow and struggled to his feet. When he got to the village gate at Li Family Stockade, he stood tall and told the cadres waiting for him at the gate: "Kill the ox!"

3. The tragedy of Spotted Leopard

"Why don't you just slaughter *me*! Boil *me* up in a pot!" In the Team Three feed yard, Old Man Li Tao held on to Spotted Leopard's halter for dear life, yelling furiously: "Whose idea is it to eat the livestock? Just eat me instead and have done with it!"

Leading the animal away, team leader Xiao Kuan replied: "Think about it, Uncle Tao—which is more important, looking after people or animals? Besides, this is a brigade decision, proposed by Brother Tongzhong!"

"Tongzhong?" Old Man Li Tao was dumbfounded. It had not occurred to him that this decision could have been made by his own crippled son. He might be head of the family, but Tongzhong out-ranked him in the official hierarchy. It looked as if Spotted Leopard's fate was sealed. "Okay, okay! Take him away. Take all the livestock away from the troughs! Clear the stock barn! We're done for!"

Old Man Li Tao did not have the heart to look at Spotted Leopard. He let go of the halter, sat down on a small bench facing the wall and began to cry. Not long after, he heard the sound of bellowing from behind the canteen. He thought it was Spotted Leopard calling out to him; it was like a knife piercing his heart. Everything in front of him went black, and he collapsed on to a pile of straw.

A few commune members carried Old Man Li Tao home. Dr. Wang from the brigade clinic hurried over, supporting himself with his cane. He pinched the pressure point between the old man's upper lip and nose so hard he almost drew blood; Old Man Li Tao finally opened his eyes and spluttered out the air that had stuck in his chest.

His daughter-in-law whispered: "Dad, are you okay?"

Father-in-law just sighed and said nothing.

His grandson Little Grain Bin climbed up onto the bed: "Grandpa, who made you mad?"

Grandfather just sighed and said nothing.

Dr. Wang led Tongzhong outside, his face grave: "He's famished. He can't cope with upset and anxiety. There's nothing I can do. Just let him rest!" Dr. Wang sighed as he thought about the ox and hobbled off with his cane.

Spotted Leopard was already down on the ground, its legs trussed. It bellowed plaintively, and tears the size of beans flowed from its big round knowing eyes. It looked despairingly at those around it, as if to say: People, don't kill me! I can still till the soil, I can still pull a plough with a seven-inch blade! If you kill me, how many meals will it provide?

Li Tongzhong could not bear to watch any longer and quietly left the slaughter yard. As he walked away, he just had to glance back. Over the raised collar of his army greatcoat, he looked at Spotted Leopard one last time. Then he pulled the padded flaps of his hat over his ears to block out the sound of its bellowing.

When Tongzhong heard that his father had collapsed, he hurried home to see him. But his dad turned away and faced the wall, ignoring Tongzhong. Tongzhong understood how much his father loved Spotted Leopard. He remembered how the year the mutual aid groups had changed into the collectives, he had taken his demobilization allowance and gone with his father to the Ten-mile Store livestock market, returning with the animal. There is a saying: "When you sell vegetables you don't sell the basket, and when you sell livestock you don't sell the halter." Tongzhong's demobilization allowance had been barely enough to buy this ox, so his father had gone to the mountain general store and picked out a length of straw rope. He joked that this was a golden halter, and with this golden halter he led the ox back from the market. As soon as he entered the village, Father had pointed to the black markings on the ox and bragged to the members of the collective: "I'm bringing home a Spotted Leopard. Look at the legs on him, they're like four pillars!" The house was cramped, and there was nowhere to put livestock, so Father had tethered it to the crossbeam in their outer room. During the night Spotted Leopard chewed through the rope and made its way into their inner room, where it ate five pounds of seed cotton and six and half pounds of seed grain, and in the process knocked over the new pot that had contained the seed grain and smashed it to pieces. "Fine! Fine!" Father stroked his beard and boasted: "He's got a powerful appetite, so he's sure to be a powerful draft animal."

When the time came to hand the animal over to the collective, Father got Cuiying to make one of the red silk sashes used in *yangge* song-and-dance performances into a giant rosette and attach it to the ox's horns. Father spread a new cotton quilt over the ox's back and paraded the animal proudly on a tour of the village, twisting and weaving through all sixteen alleys before finally arriving at the newly built stock barn. From then on he moved in with the ox, and there he had stayed for seven years, winter and summer. Even though several animals had joined them in the barn, Father always loved Spotted Leopard best. He would stroke the ox's back and say: "Socialism is a cart, and we can depend on him to pull us the first leg of the journey!"

Now Tongzhong stood at his father's bedside. He said shamefacedly: "Dad, Spotted Leopard was getting on a bit . . ."

"Don't say that, don't say that . . ." Father's beard quivered.

"Dad, next time there's a good harvest, I'll get you another one to take his place. . . ."

"Don't say that, don't say that . . ." Two streams of tears flowed from the corner of Father's eyes.

"Dad, what do you say?"

"What I say is . . ." Father struggled up, propping himself up on his arms, and stared fixedly at his son. He whispered: "Tell your dad the truth. . . . Does the Party still want us or not?" Father suddenly bit down on the corner of the quilt, his scrawny shoulders shaking convulsively.

"The Party still wants us! The Party still wants us!" Tongzhong struggled to control his emotions; sadly he added: "The Party doesn't know we're hungry. . . ."

"That's okay then, that's okay." Father struggled to a sitting position. He looked compassionately at his son and said: "Then you, as Party secretary, cannot even think about lying down. No, absolutely not. Haven't you seen? The villagers are famished, they're facing starvation, and yet not one of them has left, not one of them has complained. Why? It's because they have faith in the Party! My boy, the life and death of four or five hundred people rests with you. I know that there isn't a grain of wheat in your stomach. If the hunger gets too much to bear, think about how we survived the thirty-first year of the Republic [1942]; think about your mother, who died on the road as a famine refugee. Somehow or other, you have to get the villagers through the spring. My boy, I beg you. I beg you . . ."

Tongzhong slumped to his knees in front of his father, his eyes full of tears: "Dad, your son will remember what you say."

4. No tax on bullshit

When the beef had all been weighed out, entrails and all, there were 9.3 ounces per person. In order to get the beef into the stomachs of the commune members in a fair and equitable way, the brigade decided to share out the meat household by household. Whatever cabbage, turnips, and charcoal remained in the canteen stores was divided up along with the beef that same night, thus quietly putting an end to the system of collective dining that had been in operation for more than a year. Stoves were lit in the more than 120 peasant cottages of Li Family Stockade, and boiling water bubbled in the cook pots. Spotted Leopard, like many another old ox, was performing his final service to humanity, in more than 120 steaming pans, crocks, and cauldrons.

"I'm not eating. I can't manage it." Brigade leader Zhang Shuangxi sat cross-legged by the stove and closed his eyes as if in a trance. He pushed away the big green glazed bowl that his wife had passed to him.

His wife asked: "Who are you mad with?"

Zhang Shuangxi suddenly raised a hand and gave his face a resounding slap: "That's who I'm mad with! That's who!"

Panic-stricken, she grabbed his arm. "Oh my God! That's your own face."

"That's what I want to hit!" Zhang Shuangxi began to hit his mouth again: "I'll teach you to tell lies. I'll teach you to tell lies. . . . You falsified production figures, bringing disaster on all the villagers. . . ." This little peasant around forty years of age kept on yelling and flailing away at himself, his mouth swelling up until it looked like a kitchen scoop, and shedding tears of abject misery.

Zhang Shuangxi's thin nicotine-stained lips were not congenitally given to lying. It was in the year 1958 that he had been infected with the contagion that made brains feverish and throats itchy.

That year after the wheat harvest Zhang Shuangxi went with Tongzhong and Cui Wen to county headquarters to attend a Three Levels [brigade, commune, and county] Cadres Meeting. At that time the provincial newspaper printed a supplement (*haowai*) in red characters—Zhang Shuangxi referred to it as a "nickname" (*waihao*)—with a series of announcements about the launching of bumper-crop sputniks, places that had wheat harvests in excess of 3,700 pounds per *mu*, 5,300 pounds, and even 8,700 pounds. It proclaimed the Philosophy of the Great Leap and a Great Leap in Philosophy, according to which "The Earth Can Produce As Much As Men Dare To Demand," thus refuting in both theory and practice the various heresies of "the conservatives," "the nay-sayers," and the "let's-work-it-out-after-the-harvest-ers."

Even though the county had achieved unprecedented levels of grain production in that summer's harvest, and come up with a plan to keep the Great Leap going by raising production levels by 51.5 percent for the coming year, the county authorities were still severely criticized at a meeting convened by the District Committee for county Party secretaries, citing the following offences: Insufficient Recognition of Human Initiative; Lagging behind the Requirements of the Current Situation in Sustaining the Momentum of the Great Leap; Underestimation of the Activism and Creative Powers of the Masses; and so on and so forth.

In the face of the criticism of the District Committee and the supplement from the Party newspaper, County Secretary Tian Zhenshan and other leading comrades from the County Committee worried that they were falling badly behind. They felt that this piece of land on which they were standing, this land that was vibrating and shaking with the sounds of gongs and drums reporting joyful news, had perhaps already arrived at the time prophesied by Old Man Marx, when "all the springs of collective wealth would gush forth." They assiduously condemned their own Rightist tendencies, and, according to the quota set by the District Committee, they announced at the Three Levels Cadre Meeting a plan to Take Their Spot by meeting quotas in the first year and Cross the River by exceeding targets in the second year.

Hot-shot Party Secretary Yang Wenxiu had long since divined the will of his superiors. In his speech to the meeting he immediately declared that Ten-mile Store Commune would exceed targets in a single year and usher in the era of communism. He quoted from what was said to be a folk ballad from Ten-mile Store, which described the happy conditions under communism. Unfortunately, since the Ministry of Culture was promoting a mass movement for

A Whole Nation of Poets, and since everyone was therefore now a poet, there was no way to authenticate the author of this particular ditty, and some of its lines had been submerged in the deluge of verse. Only these few aphorisms had been fortunate enough to survive and be transmitted by Yang Wenxiu:

> We eat steamed buns, dipped in sugar,
> D'you think we're doing well or not?
> We wear wool, and boots of leather,
> D'you think we're doing right or not?
> We ride rockets, sit in spaceships,
> D'you think we're doing great or not!

On the stage Tian Zhenshan nodded his head: "Great, great!"

In the audience Zhang Shuangxi whispered into Li Tongzhong's ear: "Let's get out of here and make ourselves scarce. That way when the roof gets blown down by all this hot air, we won't be crushed!"

Li Tongzhong just sat there motionless and scowling; he rolled himself a cigarette in paper from the supplement and blew out puffs of acrid smoke like an angry steam train.

When the time came for each brigade to report its production targets to the general assembly, the cadres from the various brigades all became uncharacteristically deferential, each of them declining the invitation, and none daring to fire the first shot. Yang Wenxiu knew that Zhang Shuangxi was a good speaker who could fire people up, and since this was a time when that sort of inspirational address was needed, he called upon Zhang Shuangxi to speak. However, Zhang Shuangxi put a hand over half his face and whistled out between clenched teeth: "Secretary, I got a toothache."

Yang Wenxiu said encouragingly: "We don't need you to say too much, just get to the point. Show the right attitude." Then he led the applause: "Welcome! Welcome!"

Zhang Shuangxi couldn't get out of standing up, and once he was on his feet, he had no choice in what to say. So he coughed a couple of times, and when he'd cleared his throat, he blurted out: "To make a long story short, I've had a talk with our Party secretary and our accountant. Our brigade's lagging behind—we won't Take Our Pot in a year, and if we make it to the 'basin,' it'll only be the number two basin." To gales of laughter, he put on his most earnest and serious expression and looking up at the ceiling, he said: "And when will we Cross the River? We'll wait until we've climbed up to the rim of the Pot; we'll have a smoke, take a look around, and then we'll decide."

Even those farmers who were least inclined to laugh now joined in the merriment, tears of laughter pouring down their faces. With a solemn expression, Zhang Shuangxi sat back down on his half brick and whispered to Tongzhong: "How'd I do?"

Tongzhong prodded him with his fist and said: "The honest truth, real farmer's honesty!" But Cui Wen kicked Shuangxi's foot and gestured with his mouth at the stage. Yang Wenxiu was glowering at them, his face purple with rage, looking like someone who had just inflated a pig.[3]

Who could have foreseen it? This was how Li Family Stockade became a typical case of Rightism. As Yang Wenxiu pointed out in his concluding speech, the struggle between Taking Their Spot and Making It to the Basin was the essential manifestation of the Struggle between Two Lines at Ten-mile Store Commune; this so-called Making It to the Basin was a palpable demonstration of

---

3. After the people of that region slaughter a pig, they drop the carcass in a vat of boiling water; then they take it out and make an incision in the pig's leg, and the butcher blows air into the carcass, which swells up and makes it easier to shave off the bristles and remove the internal organs. The effort of blowing up the pig leaves the butcher with a purple face and swollen neck. Footnotes 3–5 to this story contain material provided by the author in a telephone conversation in October 2006.

small-producer narrow-mindedness, the idleness of the layabout, the vacillation of the head-shaker, and the stubbornness of the conservative. Those people who were promoting the theory of Making It to the Basin had to transform their standpoint, and the first thing they would have to do would be to make a Great Leap Forward in their ideological awareness, leaping from the Basin to the Spot.

On the way home from the meeting, Zhang Shuangxi, who usually sang on the road, became mute.

Cui Wen complained: "Brother Shuangxi, why weren't you a little bit more tactful in your speech? After all, there's no tax on bullshit."

Tongzhong said: "I'm in favor of Brother Shuangxi's speech. If the Communist Party is going to act on behalf of the people, it has to be a real stone mortar striking a real stone pestle, reality striking reality, none of that fancy stuff with words."

Shuangxi said: "In any case, from now on I'm sealing up my mouth and putting guards on my lips."

But after 1958 there were all sorts of political campaigns, which required almost daily reports on the Status of the Movement. Li Tongzhong's artificial leg wasn't as serviceable as Zhang Shuangxi's real legs, so the responsibility for making reports to the commune authorities fell like a disaster on Zhang Shuangxi's head.

At a Conference to Appraise the Patriotic Health Campaign, cadres who had just started to make a study of "public speaking strategies" spoke about achieving "cleans and shinys," or else about turning "stinks" into "fragrances." Zhang Shuangxi said to himself that it was like "burning damp kindling when it was cold, you have to blow hot air on it." When it came to Zhang Shuangxi's turn to report, Yang Wenxiu glanced over at him and said: "All right, next we'll be taking a look at how things are in Li Family Stockade."

Zhang Shuangxi suppressed the anger that had built up in his stomach and decided on his own special way to get his own back.

He gave a soft cough, and using the deferential voice of a junior officer who does not want to stand in front of anyone, he humbly said, "The Health Campaign in Li Family Stockade is still lagging quite a long way behind, we don't belong in the front ranks. But with the assistance of the leadership, and by doing our best to keep up with those who are more advanced, we have been able to get the young donkey that's just started pulling the grindstone into the habit of having his teeth brushed." This really astonished the whole audience; the reports from other brigades paled in comparison. Zhang Shuangxi saw Yang Wenxiu's expression of amazement, and the way he was discreetly pulling off the cap of his pen, and he couldn't help feeling a certain pleasure, the pleasure that comes from a modest act of revenge. At the thought of a donkey shaking its head from side to side to have its teeth cleaned, he could not stop himself from chuckling. Several dozen mouths, some bearded and some beardless, all dropped open simultaneously and began roaring with laughter.

"Silence!" Yang Wenxiu rapped the table with his pen, and demanded: "How did the donkey get used to having his teeth brushed? What did you do to cultivate this excellent habit?"

This was a tricky question. But while Zhang Shuangxi had never been in the Chinese Department at university, he was not lacking in the capacity to think in images and symbols. He responded: "Early this morning I was heading to the Team Three stock barn when I bumped into Erhang's wife heading off to her family's place dragging the little jackass with white eye patches. That donkey kept on braying *"ber-hang, ber-hang"* and refusing to go along with her. She flicked it with the whip, and it wouldn't move; then she whacked it with the whip handle, and it still wouldn't move. Erhang's wife asked the little donkey, 'Are you frightened? Are you scared?' The donkey shook its head. Then she asked it: 'D'you need hay? D'you want feed?' The donkey shook its head again. 'So what on earth is up with you?' Then the little donkey lifted up his chin toward Erhang's wife and bared its teeth. Erhang's wife was so scared she dropped her bundle on the ground and screamed at the top of her voice: '*Ai ya*! Uncle Tao, your donkey's going to bite me!' The old stockman Li Tao rushed over, and when he saw the donkey baring its teeth, he said to Erhang's wife: 'Don't be afraid, sister. He isn't going to bite you, he's upset with me because I was in too much of a hurry to clean his teeth!' Old Man Li Tao led the little donkey back, and then, with a basin of clean water and a brush, both of which had been sterilized, he brushed the donkey's upper teeth three times, its lower teeth three times, and its gums three times. Only when he'd given them enough of a brushing—three times three makes nine times, this precise number—did Li Tao hand over the halter to Erhang's wife. Then he gave the donkey a slap on the rump and said: 'Off you go.' The little donkey snorted and headed off obediently with Erhang's wife, skipping and frisking all the way." Zhang Shuangxi wiped away the beads of sweat that had formed on his nose as a result of the intensity of his creative processes, and gestured toward Yang Wenxiu: "That's how it happened."

Yang Wenxiu scribbled all of this down in his notebook, and asked: "What are the benefits of tooth cleaning for livestock?"

To this, Zhang Shuangxi applied logic and replied: "It prevents mouth ulcers and itchy tongue."

Zhang Shuangxi's report proved to be a great success. In a state of fear and trepidation he received from Yang Wenxiu an embroidered banner inscribed: "Public Health Vanguard." But as soon as he left the gates of the commune headquarters, he tucked it into his shirt. When he got home he stuffed it into a hole in the wall, and never told anyone about it.

From this point on, whenever reports were being delivered on the developments in the situation of any political campaign, it only needed Yang Wenxiu to be present, and whether it was by means of Pavlov's theories of the conditioned reflex or Newton's law of inertia, the desired outcomes would be authenticated every time from the mouth of Zhang Shuangxi. For example, in his report on the campaign to stamp out illiteracy, he said that in Li Family Stockade there was an old couple in their seventies who didn't feel sleepy at night, so the old man would write characters on his wife's back and teach them to her, going on like this until the second cockcrow. When reporting on the campaign to Eradicate the Four Pests, he told of how the cats in Li Family Stockade were mewing plaintively because there were no more mice for them to eat. However, in the wiping out of sparrows, success had been less than total: there had been one nest underneath the eaves of the former ancestral hall that had slipped through the net, and when he went up there with a flashlight to take the eggs out of the nest, all he got was a handful of sparrow shit! It turned out that the family had left home! They're clever little devils, those sparrows!

So Yang Wenxiu praised the transformation of Li Family Stockade on several occasions, and Little Tao, the secretary at the commune offices, was forever calling them on the phone: "Hello! Li Family Stockade? Is Shuangxi there? The commune has to write a report to the county authorities, and Secretary Yang specially assigns this responsibility to him and instructs him to supplement it with some real-life materials! Real life!"

Whenever Zhang Shuangxi had to respond to this kind of phone call, he would be spitting out saliva like someone who just swallowed a bluebottle. He said to Cui Wen: "Huh, you were right when you said there's no tax on bullshit." But he also urged Cui Wen: "Don't you dare tell Tongzhong about it. If he found out, I'd be surprised if he didn't beat me on the mouth with an old shoe!"

Then, the previous fall, Zhang Shuangxi had finally got the punishment for his bullshitting.

That was when he went to the commune's Production Verification Assembly. As soon as he went into the gate of the commune office compound, he saw a chart on the screen wall of the building. At the top of the chart there was the picture of a rocket, and following that, in declining order, an airplane, a car, an ox cart, and a tortoise. The heading read "Comparison Chart for Autumn Production at Ten-mile Store Commune." He thought to himself: "I'm not in such great health, and if I ride in the rocket, I'm afraid my head would spin, but it's always bad luck to sit astride a tortoise." When it came time for him to report production, he didn't want to push his way to the top, or stay right down at the bottom, he just wanted to keep in line with the upper category within the middle group, most of whom were reporting an increase in total production of a 100,000 pounds, so he came home "riding the airplane."

At the news that Zhang Shuangxi had got on the "airplane," Tongzhong was furious: "Brother Shuangxi, so you've learned to talk big as well, have you? This 100,000 pounds of pancakes in the mirror, can the workers eat them?[4] Can the Liberation Army eat them? Party Central and Chairman Mao have told us to make real efforts, not to make hollow candy men.[5] This paradise that you're going on about, who's going to be living there?"

After Li Tongzhong had let off his "artillery barrage on Sanggamyong Ridge,"[6] he rushed off to commune headquarters: "Cut our production figure down by 100,000 pounds, I'm willing to ride the tortoise." But this trip ended up taking more than ten days: there was a lock-up behind commune headquarters, and he was incarcerated there with cadres from other brigades who chose to ride the ox cart or the tortoise, condemned to spend ten days in the cell for the

---

4. "Pancakes in the mirror" refers to the local saying: "You can't ride a dappled horse [drawn] on a wall, and a pancake in a mirror can't satisfy hunger."

5. Making candy men is a local craft, in which the vendor makes a hollow human image out of sugar by inflating it, like blowing glass; the object is to make the largest possible figure with the least material.

6. Sanggamyong Ridge was the site of a 1952 battle in the Korean War.

crime of Rightism. By the time he got back, Li Family Stockade had already overfulfilled the grain requisition quota by 100,000 pounds, under the direction of a commune work team charged with Opposing Misrepresentation of Production.

Now Zhang Zhuangxi was on the hot seat again; like a man possessed, he wept and cursed: "You stupid bastard, why did you have to take the airplane!"

5. Uncle Gang and his keys

How many calories are there in 9.3 ounces of meat?

Seven days after the grain ran out, Li Tongzhong accompanied Dr. Wang on a medical inspection of all the households in the village. He discovered that of the just over 490 inhabitants of Li Family Stockade, just over 490 were suffering from edema. Dr. Wang's face darkened; he rapped the ground with his cane and said to Tongzhong: "If there isn't anything to eat in the next two days, you'd better get a special group together to go and dig graves."

The last house that Li Tongzhong visited was that of Master of the Three Halls Uncle Gang. Four days earlier, after Uncle Gang had squatted weeping in the storehouse of the communal canteen, he had returned home and fallen ill. The canteen storehouse no longer had anything raw or cooked for him to concern himself with and would never again need him to be constantly opening the door, taking out raw ingredients, putting in cooked food, weighing amounts, and keeping accounts. His life had become empty and lonely, as the spiritual pillars that had supported his old bones had collapsed. He lay on the bed, feeling the weight of his bunch of keys on his hand and gazing at them intently: "Old companions, we're going to have to part. I can't take you with me. I won't need you where I'm going. . . ."

Li Tongzhong and Dr. Wang arrived at Uncle Gang's home and couldn't help feeling sad when they saw the placard that hung over the door, reading "Martyr's Family." Uncle Gang's only son had gone off in 1944 to fight with Commander Pi [Dingjun] and had died in the Huaihai Campaign during the civil war, leaving only his parents at home. This was an old couple that deserved even more than their neighbors to live a few days without hunger!

As Li Tongzhong and Dr. Wang went into the family courtyard, they heard Uncle Gang shouting: "Hua's mother, . . . when a man dies it's like a lamp going out, why bother with funeral clothes? . . . If you really care for me, . . . just toss me a clump of cotton wadding, and let me gnaw on it . . . gnaw on it. . . ."

Hearing Uncle Gang, Dr. Wang seemed to go weak and limp; he slumped down on the stone used for beating cloth beneath the heaven tree in the courtyard and said: "I can't bear to look at this patient, I can't bear it, it's too painful to watch. . . ."

Li Tongzhong went in alone. Aunt Gang was in the process of making funeral clothes for her husband out of cotton sacks. When she saw Tongzhong, she began to cry. She brought over a stool for him to sit on and said: "Uncle's not doing well just now. He says he's lived more than sixty years, and that's enough for him. There's nothing much I'd ask for. I just think that he grew crops all his life and was in charge of the canteen for one year, if he could just have a morsel of food to chew on before he passes on. . . ."

Uncle Gang heard this from the inner room and scolded his wife: "Did you ask Tongzhong if he'd had anything to eat? Tongzhong, don't listen to her nonsense, . . . come in, I'd like to see you one more time."

Li Tongzhong went into the inner room, sat down by the bed, and took Uncle Gang's hand: "Uncle, I've managed things badly. It's my fault that you're suffering this injustice. . . ."

"I don't blame you, my boy, I don't blame you." Uncle Gang looked fondly at Tongzhong. He took the bunch of keys from his waistband and held them out: "The Party branch . . . the masses put their trust in me . . . and let me run the canteen for a year and seven months . . . and eight days. I've never been much use, I can only open the door, close the door. . . . I can't do anything much . . . can't take any of the burden from you. In the future, when there's grain again, choose someone responsible . . . give him the keys." Uncle Gang's lip quivered, and his hand trembled, as he pressed the keys into Tongzhong's hand.

Tongzhong returned the keys to Uncle Gang: "Uncle, whatever you do, you've got to get yourself through the next few days. The Party branch has written a letter to Secretary Tian—he's the one that came to us as Commissar Tian during Land Reform—and Secretary Yang from the commune will be back soon from a meeting at county headquarters. I reckon they'll be sending us grain. I'm giving the keys back to you to look after."

Then Dr. Wang pushed in through the door with a bottle of cod-liver-oil pills in his hand, and said to Uncle Gang: "Brother, this is some Western medicine that my nephew brought back from Hubei; according to Western medical thinking this is, um, nutritional, if you take a few each day, it should do you a lot more good than chewing on a cotton pad." He solemnly took the stopper out of the bottle and shook out two pills, which he pushed into Uncle Gang's mouth, took a cup of water that Aunt Gang was holding out to him, and washed the pills down.

Someone shouted outside the door: "Tongzhong, Tongzhong, quickly, quickly . . ." Before the sound had died down, Cui Wen dashed into the room, panting: "Just had a call from Secretary Yang . . . wants you to go to the commune offices . . . the grain rations . . . he's found a solution!"

It was as if a sudden flash had lit up the dingy room. As Li Tongzhong strode out of the room, Uncle Gang was already being helped by his wife to a sitting position, and the bunch of keys was once more secured to his waistband.

Dr. Wang stopped tapping the ground with his cane, and drew a circle in the dirt with it instead: "This is better than any kind of medicine!" he said.

6. "That's Chemistry for you!"

Li Tongzhong hurried over and was received by Yang Wenxiu in a small west-facing room heated by a coal fire. Yang Wenxiu took a letter out of his notebook and glowered at Li Tongzhong. "Did you write this letter to Secretary Tian?" he asked.

"Yes." Li Tongzhong glanced at the letter and saw a line of large characters written on it in pencil: "IF SITUATION AS DESCRIBED, SHOULD RESOLVE ASAP."

"Is it true that Li Family Stockade has no grain?"

"How about this, Secretary," Li Tongzhong smiled wryly, "Go to Li Family Stockade and eat the food there, the turnip broth, just for three days, I wouldn't make you eat it any longer than that."

"No matter how great your problem may be, the commune will deal with it for you." Yang Wenxiu recalled that when Tian Zhenshan had passed this letter on to him, he had eyed him quizzically, as if to say: Huh? So this is how you lead the way, eh, Hot-shot Yang? This had made him tense and irritated. Now he folded the letter and tucked it in his pocket. He said: "Even if you hadn't written the letter, the commune would have had to solve your problem; but you did write it, and it's up to the commune to deal with it just the same."

"We should solve the problem, Secretary."

"Okay, tell me, does Li Family Stockade have corn husks and sweet-potato leaves?"

"What d'you mean?" Li Tongzhong was caught off guard.

"Sweet-potato leaves, corn husks—the layers of leaf from around the ears of corn."

Li Tongzhong thought for a moment: "Most of the corn husks

have been spread over the pig pens and mixed with manure for fertilizer, but we still have sweet-potato leaves."

"Do you have lots of straw?"

"Straw?"

"Yes. Straw."

"We're not short of straw, enough for the animals to get by on until the wheat's ripe."

"That's fine, then." Yang Wenxiu looked relieved, and said to Li Tongzhong, "Come with me, I've got some things to show you."

"What things are those?"

"Things to eat."

Li Tongzhong went with Yang Wenxiu to the meeting room. There he saw the Party secretaries, the brigade leaders, and the canteen chiefs from the Willow-tree Corners, Heaven-tree Flats, and Bamboo Garden brigades, all sitting around the conference table and smoking. The commune clerk, Little Tao, had taken the blinds down from the windows and pasted red paper in their place. Now she was just putting the finishing touches on the words "GOOD NEWS," which she was writing in yellow paint with a broad brush. On the table was a row of a dozen or more white ceramic serving dishes, bearing black, brown, and dark red objects in square, oblong, or conical shapes.

Yang Wenxiu said to Li Tongzhong: "At the meeting we just had at the County Party Committee, they passed on an idea from the District Committee, calling on all communes and brigades that are short of grain to make a big push for grain substitutes. I came straight back before the meeting had ended to conduct some experiments. They've been highly successful, and they provide us with a way to resolve the grain shortage problem." He pointed to the objects on the dishes and announced several foodstuffs never before seen in the world: One Bite Crisp, a cake made of flour ground from corn husks, Can't Pull Apart noodles, made of flour ground from sweet-potato shoots, General's Helmet, a bun made of flour ground from straw, and others as well. He went through the substitute foods one by one, introducing the ingredients, characteristics, and merits of each, the agitations and irritations brought on by Li Tongzhong's Emergency Report being banished from the universe by these important nutritional discoveries.

Li Tongzhong felt as if miracles were occurring before his eyes, but his Rightist ideology caused him to have some slight doubts about those miracles, so he asked: "Are these really made with sweet-potato leaves and corn husks?"

"You don't believe me?" Yang Wenxiu picked up a One Bite Crisp, held it up to Li Tongzhong's mouth, and said: "Let me invite you to a meal, no grain ration coupons required. The great thing about it is that no ration coupons are needed."

Li Tongzhong broke off a piece and savored it carefully. His sense of smell told him that, though it was a bit sour, it didn't taste that odd: his sense of touch told him that, though it was a bit on the brittle side, it should still be possible to swallow it; his sense of hearing told him that it crackled when you bit into it, but it was made of corn husks, after all, and you couldn't expect it to be as good as standard-grade flour.[7] He felt annoyed with himself for chopping up the corn husks to put in the pig pens.

At Yang Wenxiu's instruction, Li Tongzhong sampled each of the substitute foodstuffs. He felt that the taste of the Can't Pull Apart noodles was close to ones made with real wheat, and he secretly congratulated the three brigades for keeping their sweet-potato leaves.

"Comrade Tongzhong," Yang Wenxiu said sternly: "The only solution for Li Family Stockade is to go in for substitute foods in

---

7. Literally 8–5 flour, prepared by a process in which 100 pounds of grain produces 85 of flour, the remainder being chaff.

a big way. If you seize this opportunity, a losing chess game will be converted to a winning one." Noting that Li Tongzhong's face was still clouded with doubt, he added: "There's no mystery to it: boil up the corn husks or the sweet-potato leaves, mash them, soak them, evaporate the water off, bring about a chemical change and there you are." Finally his voice turned more serious still: "The spirit of the moment is still Opposing Rightism, and we must absolutely reject the kind of lazy and cowardly thinking that feels that there is nothing that can be done to deal with the problem of grain shortage and speedily set in motion a mass movement to produce lots of substitute foods. Tongzhong, facts prove that Opposing Rightism can produce grain! It can produce food! It's a marvel!"

Li Tongzhong didn't catch the profundity of this last remark, so captivated was he by these extraordinary substitute foods. He made a request: "The best thing would be for one of the advanced brigades to send someone to Li Family Stockade, so we can all get to eat this One Bite Crisp tomorrow."

Yang Wenxiu gestured to the Party secretary of Willow-tree Corners: "Shitou, I'll leave this to you."

Liu Shitou and Li Tongzhong were old friends. The previous fall, both of them had ridden the tortoise together and served time in the commune lock-up. Liu Shitou was all agreement: "No problem, I promise you'll be able to do it as soon as I teach you."

"So let's get down to details right now." Li Tongzhong led Liu Shitou out of the meeting room and into the Party secretary's office. He pulled out his notebook, twisted the top off his fountain pen, and said: "We've got lots of sweet-potato leaves in our brigade. Tell me how we can make noodles out of them."

Liu Shitou stared at him: "How d'you make noodles? You use a starch mixture."

"You can make a starch mix out of sweet-potato leaves?"

"Why not? Everyone's fooling everyone else these days. You

can't only make noodles out of sweet-potato leaves, you can make meatballs with pig's bristles as well. That's Chemistry for you!"

Li Tongzhong felt as though a ladle of cold water had been dumped on his head, but he hadn't lost hope completely. "How about the One Bite Crisp?" he asked.

"They mixed in cornstarch fifty-fifty."

"And the General's Helmet?"

"There's no nourishment in it at all. All you're doing is wasting animal feed."

All hope was gone in an instant, like a puff of smoke. Li Tongzhong came resentfully to a halt, feeling that he'd been made a fool of. Suddenly he thought back to the time when he'd collapsed on the road when he was fleeing the famines, and when he came round, someone was tickling his nose with a stalk of grass, making him sneeze three times. . . .

"Does Secretary Yang know about this?"

"Who'd dare to let him know?"

"Have you learned to deceive people too, Brother Shitou?"

"If we don't deceive him, he'll chew us out; deceive him a little and he stays happy. What else can we do?"

"Shitou, our Communist Party can't act so irresponsibly."

Liu Shitou looked up into Li Tongzhong's eyes: "Look at me, brother, look at me, do I look like the sort of person who would tell people lies? . . . But I was born in the year of the rat, and my mother tells me I've always been timid. When I was fifteen, my brother and sister had to hold me up before I would dare to look at a dead toad. Ever since you and I were in the commune lock-up last year, I've had palpitations, my heart goes thump-thump-thump every time I see Secretary Yang. It's like someone banging on a drum. Haven't you heard what they say: 'I can take hardship, exhaustion as well, but I'm just terrified of the commune cell.' I've been scared silly by Anti-rightism!"

Li Tongzhong pulled down the earflaps on his cap. He didn't want to hear any more of this. He felt like crying, but in the end he didn't cry.

From outside the gate of the commune came the clamor of *suona* reed pipes and gongs. Yang Wenxiu and the cadres from the Heaven-tree Flats and Bamboo Garden brigades, and some musicians from Ten-mile Store, were standing on a trailer pulled by a Soviet-made tractor, heading off to the County Committee offices with their miracle foods to give them the good news.

Suddenly Li Tongzhong grabbed Liu Shitou by the jacket, shoved him and said: "Chase after them, Brother Shitou, get hold of them, get down on the ground and kowtow to them, and say let's all change, I'll never tell lies again, and you never force me to tell lies again, I beg you, I beg you, for the sake of the venerable Chairman Mao, let's change, let's change!"

Liu Shitou stared in horror at Li Tongzhong, then suddenly he slumped down, held his face in his hands and wept.

7. Blood-red fingerprints

Was he just going to head home and take his despair to Li Family Stockade? Li Tongzhong prowled back and forth in the snow in front of the commune office gates like a furious but exhausted lion. He could see more than 400 pairs of eyes gone yellow with starvation, gazing fixedly at the road leading southeast to market, waiting for their peg-legged Party secretary to come along that road with food for them, and their peg-legged Party secretary would have to tell them: "Villagers, we just have to put up with the famine because I'm too stupid to understand Chemistry. . . ."

Li Tongzhong, after your commune members haven't had any grain at all for seven whole days, what are you going to do to save them from death? Can you make wheat seedlings grow overnight, ripen in the morning, and bear grain before noon? Can you make the 100,000 pounds of grain that were taken away when they were Opposing Concealing Production grow legs and walk back to Li Family Stockade? Can you tell the commune members that the experience of the thirty-first year of the Republic [1942] proves that the sweet white soil of Trouser-crotch Gulley on North Mountain can be used as flour to make food?[8] If not, you have to harden your heart and tell them, villagers, friends, pity me, on my one leg I'm not up to the job, I can't carry this burden, everyone take up your beggar's staff, and come up with a way to survive. Then you can put your disability certificate in a glass frame, hang it on a bamboo pole, and take your wife and child to the veterans' sanatorium to beg for a bowl of food.

No, you can't, you can't. If there was no cold and famine in the world, what need would there be for a Communist Party? Communist Party member Li Tongzhong, you crossed over the Yalu River to fight the enemy and came back with one leg missing. Surely that wasn't so you could turn tail and abandon your villagers just when they need you most? Party Secretary Li Tongzhong, how many chances like today's will you have in your life to examine your loyalty to the people, to test what kind of a Party member you are!

A fire blazed in Li Tongzhong's chest. There was only one road for him to take, and it would bring serious consequences for him. Could he make it through? He didn't know. But he swung himself around and strode off in the direction of the grain station at Hillside Inn at the foot of West Mountain.

At the grain station, a middle-aged man with one arm was up a ladder, a broom handle tucked under his arm, wielding the brush

---

8. The author explains that sweet white soil is a soil found in that region which is fine in texture, pale colored, and slightly sweet to the taste. In earlier famines people had tried to eat it, with fatal results.

with his one hand, sweeping the snow off the roof of the building. His movements were so adept that it looked as if sweeping had always been a one-handed job, for which only the left hand was required.

This was Li Tongzhong's former comrade-in-arms Zhu Laoqing, the person in charge of the granary. In the battle of Daesoodong in the Korean War, when they wiped out the 38th Battalion of the American Second Division, one of them lost an arm and the other a leg. The one who had lost a leg bound the wound of the one whose arm was gone, and the one with one arm carried the one with one leg on his back to the medical station. Later they had come back home together, gone into the veterans' sanatorium, and then, because neither of them could stand a life where they were clothed and fed and did no work, one had been demobilized to work in agriculture, and the other transferred to the grain station.

"Hello there, Quartermaster." Li Tongzhong stood at the bottom of the ladder and called up, using the military title.

From the top of the ladder, a sallow face covered with stubble turned to him: "Oh, it's you, Second Platoon Leader, what wind blows you here?"

"Reporting, Quartermaster, I've come to beg for food." Li Tongzhong's expression was serious, with no indication that he was making a joke.

"What's that you're saying?"

"I said I want to borrow some grain."

"What's the big deal? Go ahead and borrow some!" Zhu Laoqing shook his head and came down the ladder. He noticed that Li Tongzhong seemed to be deathly ill, except for the fact that his eyes were gleaming with the brightness of fire. "Tongzhong, your old brother Zhu is aware of how tight food is in the villages. Well, for better or for worse I'm still an army officer, with four pockets on my jacket, and I'm guaranteed twenty-nine pounds of grain a month even in floods and droughts. Let's share a cornmeal bun together.

What d'you say? Go on, borrow some!" Speaking slowly, he led Tongzhong into the room that served as his office and his home, walked slowly over to a cupboard by the coal fire, took out half a bag of flour, put it on the table, and in a voice that sounded like a command, said "Weigh it and take it away."

Li Tongzhong pushed the bag away. "That's not enough. What I mean is, I want to borrow from the granary, 50,000 pounds."

Zhu Laoqing stood up with a jolt, as though he'd burned his backside, and stared in shock at Tongzhong. "What did you say?"

"Lend me 50,000 pounds of grain from your granary." Every word was like a grenade exploding.

Zhu Laoqing sat back down on the chair with a thump. He realized that there was nothing wrong with his ears. Making sure the door was closed, he said: "Tongzhong, are you completely crazy? We're not allowed to do that here."

"I know." Li Tongzhong threw his hat down on the table. "Old Zhu, there are more than 490 people in Li Family Stockade, and they've had no grain for seven days. All that's keeping them alive is turnip gruel. The Party gave those 400-plus people to me to look after, and I can't just watch them all starve to death!"

"Oh! . . ." Zhu Laoqing gazed dumbstruck at Li Tongzhong.

"If the people of Li Family Stockade were all idlers who had let their land go uncultivated, then I would take them all, more than 490 of them, sit them on the ridge of West Mountain and tell them to open their mouths and eat the northwest wind, and it would serve them right! But the people of Li Family Stockade are the kind who can endure hardship and exhaustion; all of them have calluses on their hands the size of copper cash, and who is there that didn't get up early and work till dark in the Great Leap Forward? They cared for those crops the same way that mothers spoil their daughters. I'm not bragging when I say that from Land Reform to today, the villagers have been singleminded in their pursuit of socialism, pouring out their sweat, every step they took leaving a deep imprint. They transformed a mountainous outpost into a food basket, and every year they drove great carts to deliver millions of pounds of grain to your granary. Even last year, when the harvest was poor, everyone still wanted to sell grain to the state, and all of it top-quality Bima Number One.[9] But someone got too greedy when they were Opposing Concealing Production and took away our subsistence food grain as well." Li Tongzhong stood up abruptly, pointed through the window to the granary, and said loudly: "There it is, it's right there, Li Family Stockade's food grain is stored there!"

"Oh!" . . . Zhu Laoqing exclaimed softly, his eyes on the granary.

"When we were at war with the Japanese, then with Chiang [Kai-shek], then with the Americans in Korea, the villagers led poor lads like the two of us on horseback with flowers on our chests and gave us to the Party, to go off and fight the reactionaries, and we came back, but there were many fine comrades who couldn't come back. Now I see those men's parents lying on their beds, saying just bring me a wad of cotton so I can gnaw on it . . . gnaw on it. . . ." Li Tongzhong made a choking sound he couldn't hold back, but he quickly took control of himself and fixed his eyes on Zhu Laoqing: "What do you say, Old Zhu, will you lend it to me?"

Zhu Laoqing replied expressionlessly: "No!" But somehow two tears coursed down the side his nose and hung from his beard. His voice remained without emotion: "This grain belongs to the state. Protecting it is like protecting my own life, and it is my duty."

"Old Zhu, give me a rope."

"What for?"

"I'm going to tie you up!"

---

9. Bima Number One was a strain of wheat developed in the 1950s by Chinese scientists.

The two old comrades-in-arms confronted each other, glowering menacingly. Flames, lethal flames, glinted and leaped in those black eyes. "Old Zhu, it's not grain I want, it's the Party's spirit of loving the people, it's the deep feelings of the Party and the people being like fish and water, it's the Party's traditions of being honest with the people and not telling them lies. The people who grew the crops think about these things, they talk about them, they're waiting for them, longing for them, so that their eyes are bloodshot from looking, but you . . ." Everything in front of Li Tongzhong went black, he felt as if the earth and heavens were spinning, and his erect figure toppled toward the ground. Zhu Laoqing hurried over to catch him, put his arm tightly round him, calling out "Second Platoon Commander!"

The one with only one arm helped the one with only one leg over to the bed. The one with one leg made a supreme effort to open his eyes, his lips trembled and he said weakly but insistently: "Lend it to me, I'll pay you back, I'll pay you back. . . ."

Zhu Laoqing soaked some biscuit in boiled water and fed it to Li Tongzhong a spoonful at a time. His voice was hoarse: "Tongzhong, we'll let the authorities know how things stand, we'll go together, one short an arm, the other short a leg."

"I let them know, brother Zhu."

"What did they say?"

"The authorities say corn husks and sweet-potato leaves can turn into grain, and we should make people who have starved for seven days eat that . . . eat that Chemistry."

Zhu Laoqing was at a loss for words. He pulled a long pipe with a jade bowl out of his pocket, sat down on his stool, and smoked one pipe after another. He felt that his heart had gone cold, and he trembled with the effort of talking. "Since I've managed this granary, there's never been the slightest thing go wrong. I've wiped out the rats the way we did with the Japs. Why? Because this is the sweat and blood of the tillers, the lifeblood of the Party. . . . I took in the grain from you people at Li Family Stockade, millions of pounds of it, but I never knew that the people of Li Family Stockade were going hungry. . . ." Zhu Laoqing wasn't particularly articulate, least of all when he was as distressed as this, and it was hard to work out what he had decided to do. "There's more than 100,000 pounds of grain in this granary, and if it hadn't been for the snow making it impossible to get through the mountains, it would all have been shipped out by now. In the West Granary there's 50,000 pounds of corn, best-quality Imperial Gold, we dried it before the snows came. This evening, when the moon has gone in, the back door to the granary will be left unlocked, and your old one-armed brother Zhu will be on duty." Suddenly he started to cough. "My lungs are no good, no good."

Li Tongzhong understood. The strength suddenly returned to his body, he rolled off the bed and said: "Brother Zhu, give me some paper, I'm going to write a Requisition Slip."

"No need to do that." Zhu Laoqing shook his head, and pointed to his heart, "I'm here, I'll know."

Li Tongzhong found a piece of writing paper on the desk, took the cap off his pen, and pondered. He wanted to write about the difficulties facing Li Family Stockade, to write about his experiences all those times he had told the authorities how things were, to write about the more than a hundred people at death's door, all swollen up with edema, but there were so many things to be said he didn't know where to start. Finally, he just wrote a few lines:

Spring shortages extremely serious, seven days without food. Commune members suffering cold and hunger. Borrowing food from grain station, matter of life and death. If breaking law, only one responsible. Relief corn to be returned next year.

Today borrowing exactly 50,000 lbs corn from Hillside Inn Grain Station.

Li Tongzhong, Party Secretary, Li Family Stockade Brigade
Feb. 7, 1960.

Zhu Laoqing put on his reading glasses and looked at the Requisition Slip, then took his own pen out of his jacket pocket and added a stroke, changing the "one" in "only one responsible" to "two." Then underneath Li Tongzhong's signature, he added in large clear printing:

Communist Party member Zhu Laoqing, Hillside Inn Grain Station

He thought for a moment, as if he had missed something, then solemnly opened his tin of chop ink, pressed his finger into the paste, and made a blood-red fingerprint on the page beneath his signature.

Li Tongzhong looked gratefully at his old comrade-in-arms, then without a word bit into his index finger.

"Tongzhong, what are you . . ."

"I'll . . . I'll use this."

Li Tongzhong made his imprint in his own blood with his index finger.

"See you at eleven o'clock tonight." Zhu Laoqing pushed two packages of biscuit into the pocket of Li Tongzhong's overcoat.

8. "Daren't eat it!"

After dusk Li Tongzhong returned to Li Family Stockade. By the time he had notified each of the teams to ready the carts, and the manager of the mill to get ready to start grinding grain, lamps were lit in every house in the village. It was as if the good news had grown wings, getting round the village in an instant: "There's to be an allocation of grain!"

"Auntie! Auntie!" Li Tongzhong shouted, reaching over a broken-down section of courtyard wall and pressing two packages into

Aunt Gang's hand. He said: "Tell Uncle he can chew on these first, and he'll be able to eat a proper meal before too long." Before Aunt Gang had a chance to see what it was he had given her, Tongzhong had already turned round and was walking back toward brigade headquarters.

Either the biscuits or the news of a grain allocation pulled Uncle Gang back from death's door. "Don't cry," he told his wife, "I'm not done this time. I reckon us old folks have still got another ten years to go." He groped his way off the bed, and seeing the lantern of the brigade headquarters next door was lit, helped himself along with his cane, and, ignoring his wife's attempts to restrain him, took hold of the keys tied to his waistband. "I'm going to listen in on the meeting," he said. "As long as I am alive, I must do what I can to serve the commune members." With that, he hobbled out of the door.

A meeting was underway at brigade headquarters. Uncle Gang quietly sat himself down on the stump of a scholar tree outside the door, just in time to catch Tongzhong talking about the process by which he had "borrowed" grain. The brigade cadres were dumbfounded, and Uncle Gang outside was dumbfounded as well. When he thought about where the grain had come from, and when he thought how tough things had been for Li Tongzhong as Party secretary, his nose tingled and he couldn't stop himself from crying.

Cui Wen stuck his head around the partially open door and asked. "Who's there?"

"It's me." Uncle Gang told himself off for disturbing the Brigade Committee members. He gripped his cane and tried to stand up, but the energy he had felt when he came over was gone.

Cui Wen held him up and said: "Come inside. What's the point of suffering out here all by yourself?"

Uncle Gang wiped his tears and said: "I think that being human is always difficult."

People helped Uncle Laogang over to the cot by the phone

where Cui Wen usually slept. Then they all took their own places and fell silent.

Uncle Gang was the one to break the silence: "Tongzhong, even if it means starving to death, we mustn't eat that grain. . . . We've never done anything illegal here at Li Family Stockade. . . . Some of you are in the Party, some of you are in the Youth League . . . and even those who aren't in the Party or the Youth League . . . we're also the grassroots masses of the Communist Party . . . even if we're starving to death we can't touch public stores." Uncle Gang looked at everyone and added: " In 'fifty-one, when Chairman Mao in Beijing caught sight of how thin our clothes were, he was afraid we were going to freeze . . . so when winter came we were issued warm clothing. . . . I had these padded trousers given to me by Secretary Tian from the County Party Committee as he is now." He prodded his padded trousers with a finger and said: "These very ones, these very ones . . . when I'm so hungry I'm going crazy, I look at these padded trousers and I think to myself . . . Chairman Mao didn't let us freeze . . . he won't let us starve . . . maybe it's like when there was a gale a couple of years back and the phone line was cut off . . . those above are cut off from those below . . . but if we wait a couple of days, and a couple of days more . . . until the lines are connected again . . ."

In places where the lamplight didn't reach, there were people sobbing and others blowing their noses.

"So let's hold off for a couple of days." Li Huangnian, the leader of Team One, knocked his pipe against the sole of his shoe, and said: "We can't make Tongzhong take on this big a responsibility for us."

"Let me speak." The voice was that of Zhang Shuangxi. For days he had felt ashamed to meet the other villagers, he had hidden away at home, and when there were meetings he would crouch in the shadows. But now he stood up in the corner, and said: "Uncle Gang, Brother Huangnian, let's go and bring the grain back while we've still got the strength to do it. If we wait a couple more days, I'm afraid we might not be capable of carrying the grain back even if they said we could have it. If just one of the 490-odd people dies of hunger, that'll be a crime that we'll never atone for as long as we live. If something bad happens to Tongzhong, then I'll . . ." He raised his hand and paused for a moment, wheezing out a breath that smelt like he'd eaten raw onions, before continuing in a hoarse voice: "Then if it means being shut in a dark cell, going on trial, being sent to labor camp, or some hardship even greater than that, I, Zhang Shuangxi, will take his place!"

From outside the window came a shout: "Uncle Huangnian, our animals won't be any use, they're just lying there and they can't get up." The voice was the Team One carter, Erleng.

"Listen to that, Uncle Huangnian." The accountant Cui Wen had already decided on a course of action. "It's not just the people that can't wait, the animals can't wait either. I think we have to eat that grain, and if the sky falls, it's up to us in the Brigade Committee to take its weight."

The other members of the Brigade Committee stood up, and said: "That's how it is."

Finally, Li Tongzhong spoke up: "Uncle Gang, I admit my guilt, and ask you to forgive me for this crime. If we borrow some grain now, we'll save people and livestock. In the future we can contribute more grain to support the state, and maybe we can atone for my crime. Just concentrate on getting ready, we'll assemble in a while outside West Gate." After a moment's thought, he added: "It's okay if I'm the only one that goes from the brigade office; Brother Shuangxi, Brother Cui Wen, you stay in the village and look after things here."

The meeting dispersed. With feelings of nervousness mixed with those of relief, the people left the brigade office. In one of the houses, a silhouette appeared on the window paper, and a sobbing voice called: "Dad, wake up . . . wake up, the grain is coming, we'll be saved!"

9. In the feed barn

In the Team Three feed barn, Old Man Li Tao had already entrusted two mules and four additional draught animals to the carter. He was filled with joy as he announced to his faithful servants who were tied up by the trough: "The grain allocation is coming. You've made it through! You've made it!"

Tongzhong, Xiao Kuan, and the Team One carter Erleng pushed the cotton curtain aside and walked in. Xiao Kuan winked at Tongzhong and said: "Uncle Tao, Look! The commune members from Team One have come to learn the scriptures from you!"

Old Man Li Tao looked around from where he stood by the trough and said: "Huh! You're here to learn the scriptures when you haven't even had a decent meal yet?" He was more than a little distrustful of the recent rage for "learning scriptures."

Erleng said, "Over in Team One we've watched the way you've kept your animals strong and healthy in the famine, so you can still hitch them up to big carts, and we can't work out what kind of magic you're using. Our team's animals aren't in good shape. We can only put together a team to pull one cart. They all told me to ask you, Uncle Tao, what are you feeding your animals?"

"What am I feeding them?" Old man Li Tao's heart felt as happy as if he were being cooled by a fan in the heat of summer. "Livestock can't speak. They have to rely totally on man to worry about them." He looked at his son and Xiao Kuan: "To tell the truth, there's a secret I kept from you cadres. After autumn when I saw that there was a shortage of grain, I saved a few handfuls of feed each day." He lifted up a pile of straw to reveal a few cloth sacks. "Here it is . . . even though this group of animals hasn't had enough feed, they still haven't missed a meal. You want to know about the scriptures? There they are."

Xiao Kuan said, "Hm, so you've kept this secret from brother Tongzhong?"

Li Tao glanced at his son and said: "He was even willing to eat the livestock, you think he'd let me keep the feed without eating it?" As he thought of Spotted Leopard, and grieved that the animal had not made it to today, he began to feel sad again. "But I can't blame you. I'm the one who looks after the livestock, so I'm going to care about them more than you do. Socialism is a cart; it depends on mules and horses to pull it forward!"

Moved, Li Tongzhong looked at his father, remembering that, in the days when the canteen was still able to provide everyone with a ladleful of rice porridge, the old man would wait until the woman delivering the food had left and then tip his serving of porridge into the animal's trough.

Xiao Kuan saw his chance and wheedled: "Uncle Tao, we're just getting ready to go and fetch the grain, but Team One's livestock aren't in good shape. . . ."

Li Tao's heart sank: "You mean you want to use our animals?"

Xiao Kuan said flatteringly: "Uncle Tao, our commune members say that if they can't use the animals you've been looking after, there's no way we can even think of bringing the grain back."

Old Man Li Tao sat back down on the pile of straw and thought for the length of time it would take to smoke a pipe. Finally he spoke up: "Can I just stand by and watch you not being able to fetch the grain? My animals aren't in too bad shape, this Sichuan horse and the black mule should be able to manage to pull a cart. Since you cadres have already made the decision, can a simple stockman like me get in the way?"

Before Old Man Li Tao had even finished speaking, Erleng had gone over to the trough to unhitch the animals.

"Hold on." Old man Li Tao tapped Erleng on the nose with his pipe: "Those draft animals of yours may be stiff and slow-moving, but you're not to use the whip too hard on quicker animals like mine."

"Uncle, take a look at me!" Erleng pulled his jacket open and pointed to the ribs protruding from his scrawny chest. "Even if you told me to wave the whip, I wouldn't have the strength to do it."

Li Tao looked soberly at Erleng's eighteen protruding ribs, nine on each side, and it really was two-nines-are-eighteen pieces of reliable evidence. He unfastened the ropes tethering the animals.

After Xiao Kuan and Erleng had led the draft animals away, Old Man Li Tao called his son back: "I hear there's quite a bit of grain, but you should remember to tell the commune members that it's better to be economical when the grain comes up to the top of the bin than when it's down to the bottom of the bin; they mustn't go crazy and lose their ability to endure." The old man sized up his son lovingly: "The last few days I've felt bad for you. When the grain's been fetched . . . ," he pointed at his son's artificial leg, "you should give that thing a good rest. Even with a stick you can't be on it all day."

"Okay, Dad, when the grain's here . . ." Tongzhong thought of something, and his expression turned sad, "This thing and I will both get a rest."

"That's right. There'll still be lots of time for you to be running around in the service of the masses." As he spoke, the father walked over to the feed trough, his hands behind his back.

10. A voice outside the gates

A line of carts, large and small, had formed on the road outside the West Gate of the village. The members of the Grain Transport Team, composed of core members of the militia, had each eaten two bowls of boiled turnips and cabbage, and joined the line standing beneath the gate.

Li Tongzhong laid down three rules for everyone: Number One, maintain discipline—when we get to the grain station, we take away what's ours and not a single grain that isn't ours; Number Two, don't ride on the carts—let the animals save their energy to pull the grain; Number Three, it's the middle of the night—don't disturb the neighbors.

The convoy set off on a mountain highway that glimmered in the snow.

"Climb up, there's no strength in that leg of yours," said a voice in Tongzhong's ear. It was Zhang Shuangxi.

"You shouldn't have come," said Li Tongzhong, a little annoyed.

"I'm going with you; even if you go to the end of the earth, I'll still be with you."

"The Brigade Committee . . . we're all going with you." The voice was Cui Wen's.

By the light of the stars, Li Tongzhong saw the figures of a dozen people, huddled together as they followed him. He sighed unhappily, turned away, and set off resolutely for the grain station.

"Don't go, don't go!" From within the village gates echoed the rasping voice of the weeping Uncle Gang. He staggered through the gate, and collapsed in a snowdrift by the road, but still he clambered and crawled, crying out: "Children, come back . . . even if it means starving to death, we mustn't touch public grain. . . ."

A gust of mountain air blew away the sound of Uncle Laogang's voice.

Li Tongzhong walked on, never looking back. He felt as if there were a small worm crawling out from the corner of his eye, a single Communist Party member's tear, which he would allow to flow only when nobody could see.

On the road there were no voices, only the clip-clop of the horses' hooves.

11. "Chairman Mao, I beg Your forgiveness . . ."

After several days of silence, the grindstones in the three mill sheds at Li Family Stockade could be heard rumbling as they ground corn. A long line of people formed outside the grain sheds. By the terms of the overnight household grain quota, every family would first receive one day's worth of cornmeal, so that everyone in the village could get a decent meal, and then they could pick up more as more was ground.

As the grindstones rumbled, Uncle Gang was moaning. After Xiao Kuan had carried him back from outside West Gate, he had been lying on his bed, caught in a contradiction he could not resolve. What could be done? Grain obtained illegally should not be eaten; but if they didn't eat the illegally obtained grain, there were people on the verge of death by starvation. You've lived sixty years, you're just about ready to be buried, and if you shut your mouth and refuse this illegal grain, you can become a blameless and law-abiding spirit. But must all the villagers, all four or five hundred of them, follow you and fill their mouths with dirt in their graves?

But in the minds of the great majority of tillers who had gone seven days without a morsel of grain, from the point of view of the essential functioning of their digestive systems and the extreme weakness of the bodies, there was no distinction at all between grain legally or illegally obtained; you could say that both were equally efficacious. Nutritionists will confirm that corn will have the same protein, starch, and calorific content no matter if it is legally or illegally obtained.

That was the reason why, in the long line that stretched in front of the village mill sheds, faces showed a smile of relief and eyes shone with the light of life. Even Uncle Gang's perennially obedient and submissive wife had taken her place at the head of the line as a member of a martyr's family, as if she were completely unaware of Gang's principles.

Illegal grain was still life-saving grain, and this divergence of the spiritual and the material caused Uncle Gang to become more and more confused. Then Cui Wen called him from outside the door: "Uncle Gang, there isn't enough space in the mill shed to pile up the grain. We need to use the canteen storeroom, the team storekeeper needs you to unlock it right away!"

Uncle Gang had to make up his mind then and there about this illegal grain. He cleared his throat, at a loss for how to reply.

"Uncle Gang, I'll be at Team One waiting for you." Without ever coming in, Cui Wen hurried off so fast his feet barely seemed to touch the ground.

What could he do? The contradiction between the spiritual and the material had left him with no way to go. He clambered down from his bed and stood up. Then he thought of something; he fumbled for a lamp and lit it, holding it up so that it shone on the portrait of Chairman Mao on the wall. Two streams of tears ran down and splattered on the square table that he had been given at the time of Land Reform. "Chairman Mao, I beg Your forgiveness this once. . . ." Through his sobs, he continued: "Our cadres at Li Family Stockade are honest farming people. They've never stolen or plundered. . . . I've watched Tongzhong grow up. He went off and fought in Korea. He's a child that has received years of instruction from You. . . . We've really got no choice but to eat this grain. . . ." Through a fog of tears, Uncle Gang looked up at Chairman Mao smiling kindly at him. He wiped away his tears and blew out the lamp.

In the darkness of the village lane, Uncle Gang tottered along on his cane, the words "forgive . . . forgive . . ." accompanied by the clinking of keys.

12. Three large cook pots

With the whole village imbued with a spirit of euphoria, Li Tongzhong and his leg slept soundly and sweetly, one on the bed and the other on the floor.

Not until the grain had been brought back without incident, the rumbling of grindstones had been heard in the mill sheds, and the commune members had started to measure out the golden cornmeal and bring it home, did Li Tongzhong suddenly feel weak and exhausted. The pain in the right side of his chest that had flared up the last few days and the sores that had developed from the chafing on the stump of his leg suddenly became unbearable. He felt that he would have to have a long sleep before he would have sufficient energy to get his artificial leg to carry him to the County Police Headquarters and turn himself in.

Cuiying was as ignorant as the other commune members of the secret behind this grain. She had cheerfully gone along with the older women and young wives to pick up her rations. She took her son Grain Bin over to the stock barn for his grandfather to take care of so that her husband could get a good sleep. In the stillness of his house, the only sound was Li Tongzhong mumbling in his sleep: "It was me. . . . I am Li Tongzhong. . . ."

It was after noon by the time Li Tongzhong woke up. The house was filled with white steam redolent with the fragrance of cornmeal buns. Cuiying was sitting in front of the stove wiping her eyes.

"Cuiying, are you . . . ?"

Cuiying set some buns and a big bowl of yellow cornmeal mush on the table by the bed: "Everyone in the village except you has eaten their fill," she said, her face turned away.

"Cuiying, are you crying?"

"Eat your food." Cuiying avoided his gaze. "The coal fire wasn't working properly, so I added some kindling, and the smoke got in my eyes."

True enough, what would be the sense in crying for a village woman who'd only just got hold of some grain and hadn't even had the time to be happy? Tongzhong picked up a bun and chewed off a few large mouthfuls. "Delicious! Delicious!" he praised her. "You're such a good cook you can make husks taste good, and this is made of best-quality cornmeal!"

Cuiying looked at him sadly, then lowered her head and wrapped another two buns in a cloth, then scraped the bottom of the cook pot with a spoon, serving out half a bowl of cornmeal mush and heading for the door.

"Cuiying, are you only taking food to Dad now?"

"He's eaten already. So's Grain Bin."

"Then where are you taking that to?"

"Don't ask. Just eat your food in peace."

"Whose family's in trouble?" Tongzhong was reaching for his artificial leg.

Cuiying came to a halt, her eyes red-rimmed. "When I went out of the village to gather firewood, I met a famine refugee. . . ."

"Famine refugee?" Tongzhong's heart sank. He understood that his wife had herself come to Li Family Stockade in the flight from famine, and her father had died of starvation in the moat around the village. He knew the hardships of the refugee. He pushed his bowl away and said: "Go on, take the food to him."

As soon as Cuiying was out of the door, Tongzhong strapped on his artificial leg.

When Tongzhong arrived at West Gate, he saw an old man with a white beard holding a cane and resting against his bedding roll, slumped against the gate. Cuiying was feeding him, a mouthful at a time. A circle of commune members surrounded the old man, pressing freshly made cornmeal buns into his battered bamboo basket. The old man recovered, straightened up, and said: "Thank you, thank you!"

Tongzhong asked: "Grandpa, where are you from?"

"Willow Corners."

This reminded Tongzhong of Liu Shitou and his "One-bite Crisp." He came to a decision: "Don't go, Grandpa, I'll scrape together some grain and give it to you to take home."

"Thank you so much." The old man pointed beyond the gate and said: "There's more than a hundred behind me. We can't all impose on you."

Tongzhong went outside the gate. He saw a silent throng moving slowly by the foot of North Mountain. Some carrying bedding rolls, some with baskets on their arms, they headed into the bone-chilling wind along the snow-covered mountain path, moving forward, moving painfully forward.

The man at the front of the line had a bedding roll over his shoulder and a small megaphone in his hand. From time to time he would turn back, put the megaphone to his mouth and yell: "Don't get out of line! Don't get out of line!"

"Shitou!" Tongzhong called out to the leader.

Liu Shitou pretended he hadn't heard. He bowed his head and didn't look at him.

Tongzhong went up to him and pulled him to the side of the road. "You're the Party secretary," he said. "Where are you taking these people?"

Shame-faced, Li Shitou responded: "Don't call me Party secretary, just call me beggar. The Party branch decided we should leave the village and beg for food, so the Party secretary has to take the lead." He glanced at Tongzhong, then pulled the hat from his head and held it out like a begging bowl and made a bow: "Do a good deed, comrade. Do a good deed, spare us a mouthful, just a mouthful. Leave something at the bottom of the bowl for us to lick. Let us who grow grain take a lick . . . just a lick. . . ." As Liu Shitou recited these lines, his eyes involuntarily went red.

Li Tongzhong seized the hat and rammed it back on his head: "Let's talk seriously! You come in and shelter from the wind, and Li Family Stockade will give each of you two bowls of cornmeal mush."

"*Ai, ai*, we daren't eat your food."

"Why?"

"It'll scare us to death if we eat it!" Shitou took another glance at Tongzhong: "Your accountant's wife is a girl from our village. She came over this morning with a couple of cornmeal buns wrapped in a cloth, and she said . . ." Liu Shitou poked Tongzhong with his elbow: "Brother, you've been to war, you have courage!"

Tongzhong said: "Whatever you say, I insist on your eating the two bowls of mush!"

Shitou said: "Heaven-tree Flats and Bamboo Garden also have a hundred or two hundred people begging for food. They'll be here in a while. Can you afford to look after us all? You may not know this, but right now, while all the commune cadres are off at a meeting in County headquarters, several thousand people from Ten-mile Store Commune alone are heading for Sleeping Dragon Ridge to hitch a ride on a train."

Li Tongzhong's mind was in turmoil. He thought to himself: "The people of Li Family Stockade aren't going to starve, but how many Willow Corners and Heaven-tree Flats can there be?"

They got back to the village gate. Li Tongzhong grasped Liu Shitou's megaphone and announced to the famine refugees of Willow Corners: "Aunts and Uncles, you have come by our village of Li Family Stockade, and we don't have anything much to give you, but you can shelter from the wind by our village gate, and we'll make some pots of cornmeal mush for you to drink before you move on." He handed the megaphone back to Liu Shitou and hobbled into the village as quickly as he could manage.

In the village lanes, farmers who had barely eaten were conferring: "Everyone can save two ounces of cornmeal, and we can give that to our neighbors who are fleeing famine!"

So three great vats were set up at the West Gate of Li Family Stockade. In the vats they cooked cornmeal porridge so thick that you couldn't stir it with a spoon and you could pick it up with chopsticks, two big bowls per person, to send the refugee commune members of Willow Corners, Heaven-tree Flats, and Bamboo Gardens on their way.

Night fell. The cold wind that blew in fiercely through the pass blew down the snow that had accumulated on the branches, and the sky was as black as an inverted dye vat. The snow had started to fall again at some stage, huge snowflakes obscuring the mass of famine refugees.

The weather forecast on the public address loudspeaker predicted gale force north winds, with lows of minus fifteen. As he thought of the refugees converging on the little railway station, Li Tongzhong's heart turned to ice.

13. How the Criminal Ringleader was apprehended

The sky was pitch black by the time Li Tongzhong returned to the village.

He had barely entered West Gate when the accountant Cui Wen rushed up to him in a state of panic and tried to push him back out of the village: "Run! Run! The police are here!"

Li Tongzhong asked calmly: "Has the cornmeal all been shared out?"

Cui Wen stuffed a small package of money and grain coupons into Li Tongzhong's coat pocket and kept pushing him: "Don't worry about that. Just run! I'll go to court for you. . . ."

With some difficulty, Li Tongzhong extricated himself from Cui Wen's grasp and hobbled on with large strides into the village.

There was a sound of footsteps, and three figures came running over.

Li Tongzhong went up to them and asked: "Comrades, are you looking for Li Tongzhong?"

"Where is he?"

"Here." Li Tongzhong pointed to himself. "He's here."

The three men were caught by surprise. They were comrades from the Crime Squad of the Public Security Bureau. They hadn't expected that this "Criminal Ringleader, inciting the plunder of state grain" would give himself up to the law so peaceably, even cordially.

In the beam of the flashlight trained on Li Tongzhong, they saw a haggard but honest face and narrowed eyes that shone with an expression of calm and amiability.

A piece of paper, like a white face devoid of expression, flashed in front of Li Tongzhong: "Here's the warrant for your arrest."

"Hands!"

Li Tongzhong dutifully held out his hands. As the hard icy metal clamped over his wrists, he said to the brigade accountant slumped limply against the village wall: "Remember to tell Brother Shuangxi to keep enough for seed grain. . . ."

From the village lane came the sound of raised voices. Li Tongzhong frowned slightly, then gestured toward West Gate with his chin, saying to the policemen: "We can go out this way. The road is clear." He led the way to the gate.

"Don't arrest him! Don't arrest him!" Zhang Shuangxi ran up like a madman, shouting: "Take me instead! Take me instead!"

Commune members thronged out of the village lanes, forming a human tide, surging like floodwater, accompanied by the sounds of cries of alarm and tears of grief:

"We have to protect him! We have to protect him!"

"Li Family Stockade can't do without him!"

The police comrades paused in alarm, but quickly recovered

their composure and blocked the entrance to the gate. The head of the police squad shouted: "Comrade commune members, we're here under orders to make an arrest. If you want to make a protest, go to the court and report it there. Don't get out of hand! Be on your guard for bad people making trouble!"

The human flood surged on toward the gate. Grain Bin clambered onto Xiao Kuan's shoulders and shouted: "Dad! Dad!"

Li Tongzhong turned back and walked toward the crowd. The people suddenly fell silent.

"Neighbors, go home." The criminal Li Tongzhong gave his farewell speech as if he were just having a normal conversation. "Go home, all of you. It's snowing, and it's pretty cold. The comrades from Public Security are making a legal arrest. We have to respect regulations, and we don't want to make trouble for these comrades, do we? Party and Youth League members have to take the lead, members of the Brigade Committee have to take the lead, help the elderly to get home, look after yourselves, and make sure not to delay the spring plowing. I'm going to report to the authorities. Maybe I'll be back soon, maybe I'll be back for harvest in the autumn. . . ."

People stood obediently by the gate, motionless. Tears streamed down gaunt faces.

Li Tongzhong saw his wife Cuiying staring dumbly at him, Cuiying pushed forward by the crush of people, suddenly closed her eyes and collapsed against the shoulder of Fourth Aunt Li.

"*Ai, ai, ai, ai,*" Uncle Gang was sobbing, banging his head against the village wall. "God in heaven, how can this be happening? How?"

Snowflakes danced wildly in the north wind. The snow-covered roadway echoed with the *ker-chunk, ker-chunk* of a man walking on an artificial leg. Looking into the blackness where the wind was coming from, Li Tongzhong thought of the station at Sleeping Dragon Ridge, and the coldness in his heart sank to below freezing.

14. The accomplice and the Party secretary

Even before Li Tongzhong turned himself in, things had started to happen.

That afternoon, when the County Grain Commission ordered the transfer of 100,000 pounds of grain from the Hillside Inn Grain Station, Zhu Laoqing had loaded 50,000 pounds onto trucks and handed the Requisition Slip for the borrowed 50,000 to the director of the County Grain Commission. After that, he shaved and dressed in his faded army uniform, with the jacket buttoned up to the collar, the cap pulled down to within an inch of his eyebrows, and the end of the empty sleeve tucked into his pocket, as if he were preparing to attend an important occasion.

The Requisition Slip with its two blood-red thumbprints had been delivered into the hands of County Party Secretary Tian Zhenshan. Tian Zhenshan simply could not believe his eyes. He stared at Li Tongzhong's name, recalling the militia chief who had been among the first to join the army, recalling how, after demobilization, he had limped over to County Committee headquarters on that artificial leg to see him, and then how the news had come from Li Family Stockade of Li Tongzhong leading the way to start an agricultural cooperative and to cut through the mountains and bring water to the village. In the last couple of years, not only had he not seen Li Tongzhong, he had actually had very little to do with cadres below the commune level. What could he do? There are only 360 days in a year, and last year he had spent 294 days at meetings, and that didn't include little half-day meetings. What could he do? Party secretaries had to be in command of every aspect of work! He smiled wryly when people called him the "secretary of meetings"; it was true what they said: "Taxes under the Nationalists, meetings under the Communists." What could he do? Whenever he did manage to set aside the time for a trip down to the villages, he found himself having to "head down in a pretty straight line, stay on highways for most of the time, look through windshields to take in the view, have your lunch at the commune HQ." Never could he have guessed that when he hadn't seen Li Tongzhong for so long, Li Tongzhong's Requisition Slip would suddenly appear before him. His mind was a blank, and in the storehouse of his memory there was only the thought that there must be some connection between the Emergency Report Li Tongzhong had sent him and this Requisition Slip. But only the day before, Yang Wenxiu had come to the County headquarters specially to report to him that the grain shortage issue in Li Family Stockade had been resolved in a satisfactory and timely fashion. He had even declined the quota set aside for Ten-mile Store Commune from County emergency relief supplies, expressing his desire to promote the communist spirit and help those communes and brigades that were in difficulty.

"Can they really have been so lawless?" Tian Zhenshan asked the director of the County Grain Administration, waving the Requisition Slip in front of him.

"Whatever happened, the Grain Station *is* empty."

"Who's this Zhu Laoqing? How's he behave usually?"

"Disabled veteran, left an arm behind in Korea, been in charge of the Grain Station six years, usual behavior . . . how can I describe it? . . . let me put it this way, he does a better job than people with two arms."

"Eh?"

Zhu Laoqing was brought before the secretary of the County Party Committee. "Farmer in military uniform" was how Tian Zhenshan summarized his first impression of this accomplice in crime. The accomplice was standing uncomfortably before him, stiffly to attention, saluting with his left hand.

Tian Zhenshan told him to sit down, showed him the Requisition Slip and asked: "Did you and Li Tongzhong do this together?"

"People are iron and food is steel, Chief, everyone has to eat. . . ."
Zhu Laoqing remained stiffly at attention. "Li Family Stockade had
been out of grain for seven days, Chief, that's the truth, out of grain
for seven days."

"Out of grain for seven days? Is that possible?"

"Li Tongzhong wouldn't fool you, Chief. If you said to him:
'Second Platoon Leader Comrade Li Tongzhong, go over and cap-
ture Hill 250, and take control of the commanding elevation,' he'd
say, 'Yessir'! If you said to him: 'Second Platoon Leader Comrade
Li Tongzhong, tell me a lie,' he'd say: 'Reporting, my father never
taught me how."

Tian Zhenshan looked searchingly and admiringly at this
accomplice in crime, told him again to sit down, and asked: "So you
and Li Tongzhong go back a long way?"

"A long way, a long way." Zhu Laoqing continued, "Went to war
together, got wounded together, came home together, wrote that
slip together, Chief."

"You're the manager of the grain station. You realize this is a
criminal action?"

"Yes, Chief, I understand, but people are iron, and food is steel,
. . ." Zhu Laoqing was planning to offer some more profound philosophical insights, but in the end he couldn't come up with them.

The secretary of the County Committee stood up, and said, not
without distress: "For a Party branch secretary and the manager of a
grain store to . . ." he chose a relatively restrained way to express it, " . . .
for them to act without authority to appropriate state grain, and in
horrifyingly large quantities, this is a very grave matter! The tribunal
decides that they should be arrested in accordance with the law!"

"Right, Chief, right!" Zhu Laoqing stood ramrod straight and
nodded his head, to show his complete agreement. When he was
about to be led away, he did not forget to stand to attention and
salute with his left hand.

15. Li Tongzhong's confession

Following a directive of the County Committee, the County Court decided to carry out the first interrogation of the Inciter to Plunder State Grain Supplies that very night. As the secretary of the County Committee himself wished to attend the interrogation, this added considerably to the gravity and confidential nature of the case.

A row of chairs was added to the interrogation room. Tian Zhenzhan, the head of the Court, the presiding judge, and other judicial officers had already taken their seats. Yang Wenxiu, the major figure in the ongoing meeting of cadres at the County and Commune levels, had cut short his concluding speech on "Experience with the Pilot Project on Substitute Foodstuffs" to come and sit in on this interrogation. This case that had suddenly arisen had destroyed his feeling of infatuation with himself as the victor announcing his triumphs to his audience; he sat on a chair in a corner by the wall, in a state of bafflement and alarm.

"You saw Li Tongzhong yesterday afternoon?" Tian Zhenshan continued his conversation with Yang Wenxiu.

"Yes. He's a master of pretense; he expressed himself very satisfied, very enthusiastic, about the substitute foods. I didn't see any indication that he was planning a crime."

"What a strange man! What a strange thing for him to do!" Tian Zhenshan sighed over and over.

The interrogation was about to begin. The criminal had been brought directly from Li Family Stockade. Although the officers of the Crime Squad escorting the prisoner had shown concern for him with his artificial leg and had managed to get hold of a tractor for him to ride on for the journey across the commune, he was still utterly exhausted by the time he arrived at the court. Well before he reached the interrogation room, the sound of his slow and heavy footsteps echoed *ker-chunk ker-chunk* on the cement floor of the long corridor.

The door of the interrogation room suddenly swung open. The criminal, erect and gaunt, his face covered in black stubble, appeared before the judges. He leaned his shoulder against the doorway, panting, his weary eyes looking around the interrogation room and lighting on the solitary chair placed before the judges' bench. Realizing that this was his place, he walked laboriously over to it; then, when he got to within a couple of feet of it, he reached out his hand and leaned on the back of the chair as he dragged his artificial leg over, shuffled his feet into position and straightened up, ready to take his seat. At that moment he caught sight of the County Committee Secretary Tian Zhenshan; surprised, he murmured "Commissar Tian?" using his title from the Land Reform era. His eyes glinting with astonishment and delight, he suddenly reached out with large hands that were manacled together and pleaded: "Commissar Tian, save the peasants!" Then his upright but emaciated body collapsed with a crash in front of the judges' bench.

The judges were taken aback by this unexpected turn of events. With a crunching of tables and chairs, the interrogator ran over to the interrogated, Tian Zhenshan's heart pounding wildly as he held the criminal close to him, bellowing: "Tongzhong! Tongzhong!"

Li Tongzhong opened his bloodshot eyes wide, and his cracked lips moved: "Commissar, go quickly . . . Sleeping Dragon Ridge railway station . . . hurry, hurry . . ." Then, as if he had completed some sacred duty, Li Tongzhong sank into a peaceful sleep.

A cold wind rattled the windows of the interrogation room, snowflakes the size of feathers swirling silently.

16. Sleeping Dragon Ridge station

What was happening at Sleeping Dragon Ridge? Not one of the county or commune cadres currently engaged in "foodstuff chemistry" research could explain. The County Committee decided to suspend this innovative scientific investigation for the time being. With Tian Zhenshan in front, they drove straight over to Sleeping Dragon Ridge.

Tian Zhenzhan was the first to jump out of the car when they arrived at the small station with its two waiting rooms. There he saw famine refugees crowded into the dimly lit waiting rooms, in the food stalls and the tea huts where no fires were lit, on the open platforms where the wind howled, and on either side of the tracks piled a foot high with snow, all of them waiting to hitch a ride on the train. Wrapped in quilts or covered with sheets, they huddled motionlessly as if frozen to the spot by the bitter cold, only the lamplight and the snow piled on them revealing the outline of their bodies.

Tian Zhenshan came to a halt by one of the food stalls and asked: "Neighbors, where are you going?"

They were silent, pondering, "Where *are* we going? Who knows! We'll go wherever there's something to eat, and we'll find out where that is when we're on the train."

Tian Zhenshan went over to the door of the waiting room and asked: "Neighbors, what commune are you from?"

All were silent, thinking to themselves, "If we're fleeing famine and begging for food, how can we fly the flag for our commune? It's humiliating, humiliating!"

Tian Zhenshan stood under the lamplight at the entrance to the station and shouted: "Commune member comrades, wake up! We're cadres from the county and the communes; we've come here to see you. . . ."

The silent crowd began to come to life. At the door of a small food stall, Liu Shitou was sitting on an overturned basket, and he poked his head out of his quilt. When he recognized the person standing at the entrance to the station as County Committee Secretary Tian Zhenshan, he hastily pulled his neck back and wrapped himself tightly in his quilt again. But somebody pulled the quilt down a little and asked softly: "Aren't you Liu Shitou?" Liu Shitou uncovered an eye, looked out, and was shocked to see that it was Yang Wenxiu. The hand that held the corner of the quilt involuntarily lost its grip, and the quilt fell to the ground, revealing him without any cover. He hurriedly stood up and said: "Yes, Secretary Yang, it's me." Yang Wenxiu glanced at him nervously and angrily, then suddenly pushed him back down onto the basket and covered him with the quilt. "Oh, hell! How's he going to punish me now?" thought Liu Shitou to himself as he huddled motionless under the quilt, his heart pounding. He heard the crunch of footsteps coming over to him and felt more and more nervous.

"Who's this?" That was Tian Zhenshan's voice.

Yang Wenxiu cleared his throat: "I don't know him."

But just as Yang Wenxiu was speaking, Liu Shitou sprang up again like a jack-in-the-box and stood before Tian Zhenshan like an animated flour sack. From inside the quilt wrapped around him came his timid voice: "I'm Liu Shitou."

"What?" Tian Zhenshan asked Yang Wenxiu. "Liu Shitou? Liu Shitou from Willow Corners?"

Before Yang Wenxiu had a chance to respond, Liu Shitou answered: "That's me! That's me!" Feeling both nervous and proud that the County Committee secretary actually knew his illustrious surname, his esteemed given name, and his place of domicile, Liu Shitou stuck his head out of the quilt and said: "Secretary Tian, I'm not trying to damage the reputation of the county, it's just that with food grain being a bit short, we've had to bring some people out so that the ones left behind can have something to eat. If we'd all stayed at home, it would have been like two people trying to get under one quilt. If this one's covered, the other one won't be. Anyhow, we'll be back when the wheat ripens, and there'll be no delay of the summer work."

Tian Zhenshan had already thought of a painful question, but he still wanted to make sure. "Comrade Liu Shitou, weren't you having a lot of success with the substitute foods?"

"I have a confession, Secretary Tian." Liu Shitou spoke nervously, thinking that Secretary Tian was aware of the truth about the substitute foods: "I've lived to the age of forty, and I've only ever told this one lie. I know that lies can't fill your stomach, but I was scared that because we couldn't make those substitute foods I'd be guilty of Rightism again!"

Tian Zhenshan was silent in his grief, and the county and commune cadres all grieved silently with him. Only this afternoon at the conference, they had made a detailed accounting and come up with a most encouraging figure: the sweet-potato leaves and corn husks in the whole county were the equivalent of 30 million pounds of grain!

The sound of the train whistle echoed in the distance. Tian Zhenshan felt the earth shake, and he felt the foundations on which he had based all his decisions over the past two years and more shaking as well. Those figures for production increases that were precise to the third figure beyond the decimal point, those pieces of good news delivered almost daily and the deafening banging of drums and gongs in celebration, those Situation Reports that compared successes and shortcomings as "nine parts of the one and one part of the other," all of them burst like soap bubbles when subjected to the implacable test of the little station crowded with commune members fleeing from famine.

Tian Zhenshan took the small megaphone that was hanging around Liu Shitou's neck, stood on the upturned basket, and shouted: "Comrade commune members, I'm County Party Secretary Tian Zhenshan. . . . You can blame me for poor leadership, blame me for being too remote from you, for making you come to this place to flee from famine carrying your baskets on poles through the wind and snow. . . ." Tian Zhenshan's voice became husky. He jumped down from the basket, took a begging bowl from the hands of an old man with a white beard, and held it aloft. He went on: "Now, I ask you all to go back home. I'll take this begging bowl back with me, I'll hang it in the courtyard of the County Committee offices, so that we can all take a look at it, and think about how we're going to get through to the harvest, how we're going to get grain to feed the people who grow it."

People stiff with cold and hunger began to move. Soft voices, sporadic but filled with hope, brought the station back to life. The old man with the white beard held on to his cane and stood up in the snow, murmuring to himself through his tears: "All right then, I'll go, I'll go back home. . . ."

Yang Wenxiu was squatting in the snow behind the food stall. His cigarette lit up a face full of despair and terror, twitching convulsively. He was thinking: "Two years of work, all wasted, and it's all because of that hothead Li Tongzhong and that troublemaker Liu Shitou! . . .

17. In the emergency room

In the emergency room of the county clinic, Li Tongzhong had been sleeping peacefully for three days.

On the orders of the County Committee, the county clinic was doing all it could to save the life of Li Tongzhong. Because there was no longer any concern about improper conduct on the part of the comatose criminal, the cold hard handcuffs had been removed from his wrists. But all of this was carried out on the basis of "release due to infirmity"; from a legal point of view, Li Tongzhong was still a prisoner in shackles.

Li Tongzhong, do you know what has happened in the last three days? All twenty-nine grain stations across the county have been opened, and the grain that had not been shipped out because the mountain roads were cut off in the blizzard has been distributed to the cold and starving mountain villages. Cooking smoke is rising, and spring is on its way. But who could have foreseen this? Tian Zhenshan was dismissed from his post this afternoon and summoned to the District Committee offices for investigation and criticism. His offenses were listed in an emergency dispatch: "Contravening Party Discipline and State Law, Raising County Grain Distribution Quotas without Authority, Appropriating Grain Reserves, and Disrupting Purchase and Allocation." Tian Zhenshan felt distressed and regretful, not because of the dispatch, but because he no longer had the power to alter the fates of Li Tongzhong and Zhu Laoqing.

Before going to District Headquarters, Tian Zhenshan stopped by the county clinic to say his farewells to Li Tongzhong. As he came up to the bed, he saw that Li Tongzhong was sleeping soundly; perhaps he was immersed in some dream or another, because his dark eyebrows were frowning slightly, but there was still the trace of a smile around the corners of his mouth. Tian Zhenshan held one of those large hands, which was icy but firm, and called to him softly: "Tongzhong! . . ." Then he paused—what was there to say to him?

A doctor whispered to him: "He's in a coma. He can't hear you."

"No, doctor!" This was from the choking voice of a young woman.

Tian Zhenshan looked over into a corner of the room and saw Cuiying and a boy sitting on a bench. He recognized her as Tongzhong's wife and the head of a *yangge* dance troupe at the time of Land Reform. The boy was a stranger to him, but he knew those dark and stubborn eyes.

"He's been waiting for you for three days, and calling for you." Cuiying sobbed. He didn't want his father or mother, he wanted you,

Commissar Tian. Say something to him, he can hear you, I know he can!"

Tian Zhenshan's heart trembled fiercely, and it was a long, long time before he could bring himself out of his grief. He said to the man who could not hear his voice: "Tongzhong, I've made you wait too long. But you have to wait longer, wait longer, the Party will certainly correct its mistakes, just wait. . . ." Tian Zhenshan suddenly felt something. He shook that icy hand and called out: "Tongzhong, Tongzhong . . ."

"Tongzhong, Tongzhong!" Shuangxi, Cui Wen, and other commune members from Li Family Stockade shouted as they burst in to the room.

The head of the clinic pushed his way through and handed Tian Zhenshan a death certificate on which was written: "Malnutrition and exhaustion leading to edema and jaundice."

Li Tongzhong had left them, left them so suddenly. He was only thirty-one, born in the year of the dragon.

The ward was filled with the wailing of the farming people. Uncle Gang beat his head against the side of the bed and berated the heavens in anguish and incomprehension: "God in Heaven, why? Why?"

Tian Zhenshan stood by Li Tongzhong's body for a long while, tears in his eyes, paying silent tribute. When he saw the child holding the artificial leg, tears pouring down onto the leg, he thought to himself: "Those of us who have both our legs, shouldn't we be walking the road a little better than we are?"

18. People, remember

As the jeep sped along the mountain roads, Tian Zhenshan's mind surged like floodwater.

History is a Yellow River, washing its way east. But the Yellow

River is muddy, it contains massive quantities of silt, it needs a long time to come clear. Would nineteen years be enough?

Tian Zhenshan remembered that shortly after Li Tongzhong's death—maybe it was Uncle Gang who told him—the phone line that had been cut off by the storm was restored, so that the Party Central Committee found out about this terrible famine and took forceful measures to remedy it. The District Committee halted the investigation into Tian Zhenshan and sent him off to be manager of a state farm. But the conclusion to the investigation still read: "Raising county grain distribution quotas without authority and using state grain reserves without receiving approval remains an organizational error." Tian Zhenshan had no misgivings about that. But what did sadden him was that he had heard that when people had called for the rehabilitation of Li Tongzhong, his case had been set aside, because it was a legal issue, and because Li Tongzhong was now a "person from the past." The other accused in the case, Zhu Laoqing, had been released, but as to whether that was an acquittal, or merely release because he had been forced into complicity, the court declined to say. Probably because it was no longer appropriate for him to be entrusted with looking after a state granary, he was seen with his empty sleeve flapping and his long pipe with its jade mouthpiece, busy delivering food to the cadres in the County Grain Commission. As for Yang Wenxiu, he was said to be suffering from schizophrenia and sent to a sanatorium at Cockscomb Mountain to recover. Tian Zhenshan sent him a copy of the book, *How to be a Good Communist*,[10] as a way of offering encouragement, but to his regret he never heard back from him.

Now Li Tongzhong and Zhu Laoqing had both been rehabilitated. Did that offer Tian Zhenshan some consolation? He pon-

---

10. A manual for thinking and behavior written by Liu Shaoqi, the Chinese head of state from 1949 until 1966, when he was condemned in the Cultural Revolution. Liu died in prison in 1969, but was posthumously rehabilitated just before *Li Tongzhong* was written.

dered the wording of the rehabilitation decision again and again: "Notwithstanding that the methods employed by the two comrades Li Tongzhong and Zhu Laoqing were detrimental to the enforcement of the law, however . . ." However, however! Tian Zhongshan believed fervently that another kind of law should be created, aimed at those who boast, or who force others to exaggerate, those who set high quotas or impose high requisitions, or who by other means violate the interests of the peasants and refuse to mend their ways; they too should be punished according to their offences. Yes, he thought bitterly, there should be that kind of a law!

The jeep roared on, jolting as it went through the pass in the mountains to Li Family Stockade, that place so dear to him, but yet so unfamiliar, lying peacefully in that mountain valley. A flow of people converged in streams from all sides on a spot at the foot of West Mountain slope. The ceremony of rehabilitation was about to begin. Tian Zhenshan's eyes lighted on a grave mound at the bottom of West Mountain, a grave mound set off by tall straight evergreens, pines and cypresses. His eyes misted when he saw the offerings of food and the pure white wreaths that the farming people were laying in front of the grave.

"Remember the lesson of history!" Tian Zhenshan murmured to himself. "Overcoming the enemy requires a price in blood, and overcoming our own mistakes often requires a price in blood as well. Those who live should strive to gain greater wisdom at a lesser cost!"

Translated by John Shook, Carmen So, and Aaron Ward, with Richard King

GLOSSARY

....

Big-character posters. Hand-written expressions of opinion, usually posted in areas designated by the authorities, often expressing dissatisfaction with officials or policies. During the Cultural Revolution, big-character posters were used to denounce leaders at the national or local level, often in campaigns orchestrated by other leaders. This form of expression was banned in the early 1980s.

Blooming and Contending. The Hundred Flowers campaign was launched by the Communist Party in 1957 with the slogan "Let a Hundred Flowers Bloom, Let a Hundred Schools of Thought Contend," in an apparent invitation to air divergent opinions. Many of those who expressed views critical of the Party were subsequently denounced as Rightists, removed from their positions, and barred from public life. The Hundred Flowers and Anti-rightist campaigns were principally directed towards urban intellectuals, but they had an effect in the villages as well: Blooming and Contending meetings in rural areas were designed to encourage activism for state policies; those condemned as Rightists in the countryside included people who had opposed collectivization or failed to commit themselves to unrealistic production targets.

Four Pests. A mass campaign was launched early in the Great Leap to eradicate vermin; the pests were rats, flies, mosquitoes, and sparrows. The killing of sparrows disturbed the ecological balance of the villages and, like many Great Leap initiatives, was subsequently abandoned.

High-yield plot. A piece of land designated for experiment or particular attention, with a view to achieving (and then reporting) exceptional advances in food production.

Iron and Steel Battalion. A group of peasants redeployed from agricultural work to mine ore, cut timber, build furnaces, and thereby produce materials for urban factories, as part of the Great Leap campaign to produce steel.

Kang. The basic system for domestic heating in rural north China; a brick platform for sleeping on, heated from beneath by a fire lit outside the house.

Land Reform. Following communist victory in the civil war, land was taken from landlords and divided, with other property, among tenant farmers and poor or landless peasants, in accordance with a promise by the Communist Party to provide tillers with their own land. That land was taken out of private ownership within a few years in a process of collectivization that culminated in the formation of the People's Communes.

Learning the scriptures. A popular Great Leap expression to indicate studying the techniques of those individuals or organizations reporting the highest achievements.

Liberation. The term customarily used in the Mao era for the communist victory of 1949.

Masses. The political term for that majority of the Chinese people regarded as the constituency of the Communist Party and its source of support.

Nation of poets. An official campaign to write "new folk songs" was used to promote enthusiasm for the Great Leap. Millions of poems were collected in the late 1950s, written by workers, peasants, and sometimes by the local officials charged with seeing that quotas for poems were met or surpassed.

People's Commune. The People's Communes, the largest units of social organization in the countryside during most of the Mao era, were introduced in the late 1950s though a mass mobilization as part of the Great Leap. Communes were responsible for agricultural and other production, military preparedness, and social welfare. Typically comprising thousands, or tens of thousands, of peasant households, communes were divided into **production brigades**, which were in turn subdivided into **production teams**, each level with its own management and political structures. The pre-existing administrative divisions of **district, township,** and **village** overlapped with, but were not completely replaced by, **communes, brigades,** and **teams**. The formation of the People's Communes was the final stage in the progress made during the 1950s towards collective farming; they followed the earlier **co-operatives** of a few households and larger **collectives.** The communes were disbanded in the early 1980s in the post-Mao economic reforms.

Poor and lower-middle peasants. These were the groups defined by the Communist Party as the most revolutionary when the Party designated class status to villagers at the time of Land Reform. The two were generally joined together in political documents to the point where "poor and lower-middle" was a single category. Those who had been slightly more prosperous and were designated **middle peasants** were tolerated but considered unreliable, while **rich peasants** and **landlords** saw their land and other property taken from them and distributed to their poorer neighbors. The class designations made at the time of Land Reform remained in effect through the Mao era.

Sputnik. The launching of the first Soviet satellite, or sputnik, in 1957 was seen as a triumph for socialism, and initiatives in Chinese public life, such as the establishment of the canteens or advances in the production of grain and steel, were sometimes referred to as "launching a sputnik."

Work record. Under the People's Communes, labor performed by each individual was not immediately paid, but was recorded as work points, which would result in payment derived from collective income.

Yangge. A traditional form of popular local entertainment in northern China that was adopted by the Communist Party in the 1940s as a vehicle for public celebration and education. *Yangge* performances consisted of simple lively dances, sometimes accompanied by brief dramatic sketches.

ABOUT THE EDITOR

....

Richard King is director of the Centre for Asia Pacific Initiatives and associate professor of Chinese in the Department of Pacific and Asian Studies, University of Victoria. His research is on twentieth-century Chinese literature and the arts, particularly from the Mao era, and Asian popular culture. He has translated the work of a number of contemporary Chinese authors, including *Snake's Pillow and Other Stories: Tales from Jiangnan* by Zhu Lin (1998) and *Chaos and All That*, a novel by Liu Sola (1994). He is also the editor of *Art in Turmoil: The Chinese Cultural Revolution, 1966–1976* (2010), and *Global Goes Local: Popular Culture in Asia* (2002, with Timothy J. Craig).

PRODUCTION NOTES FOR

. . . .

King / *Heroes of China's Great Leap Forward*
Cover and interior design by Julie Matsuo-Chun
Display type in Memphis; text in Warnock Pro
Printing and binding by Sheridan Books, Inc.